I0671644

Hardman

Samantha Fontien

Hardman

ISBN: 0993473512
ISBN-13: 978-0-9934735-1-7

DEDICATION

Thank you, to my 'Amazing PA'. *Laura Smith*. How lucky I was to meet you. You're extraordinary, honestly awesome. Love you HARD Gurl.
Krissy V, thank you for being my Friend, I'm *truly* blessed to have you walking this journey with me, my gorgeous travel buddy.
Thank you to *L Chapman*, who takes friendship to the highest levels and beyond… Love you gurl <3
Jennifer Foster, my Music Fairy, how I adore you and your magical tunes, you're inspirational.
Krista Webster, how you make me laugh like no-one else does, you saucy minx. (And you pick out lovely bikini's too, thank you for that. Hahaha)
Jade Jez, from steampowerstudio's, what can I say, only how I LOVE my cover. Your talent is just beyond amazing.
Thank YOU. Xx
http://www.steampowerstudios.com.au/.

And thank you to all my friends for your friendship, you make life so much easier.

… A HUGE thank you also, to *Maria Lazarou* for coming to my aid and for your help in putting this book on Goodreads for me, you're a hero.

Thank you to all the lovely readers for your support, you ROCK!!

Hardman

CONTENTS

Hardman

Hardman

Published by 2 Librans Publishing

Samantha Fontien

Samantha Fontien

<u>GLOSSARY</u>

Bint – Dozy girl. A pretty air-head. A sex object/receptacle.

Claret – In this case, NOT wine, but UK slang, meaning blood.

Score – Slang for situation, not as in a sports result or goal; to know all the important facts in a state of affairs, especially the unpleasant ones.

Sort – Very pretty woman. A raving sort would be extremely gorgeous.

Rep – Reputation.

Miffed – Upset. Bugged. Irked.

Firm – A well organised Gang or crew. A group of football/soccer hooligans, usually made up of 200-300 people, but the better firms, have far more than that number. Or a name given, to a large gang involved in organised crime. In this case, it's a mixture of both. Run by the top ranking officials, movers and shakers called **Face/s or Gov's**.

Estate – A council housing estate is the British equivalent to the projects in America. They are affordable, local government housing. Built as either tower blocks or smaller four floors buildings or a cluster of houses set in groupings, reproduced repeatedly on the plot/site/land.

Kerb – The line of stone or concrete forming an edge between a pavement and a roadway. USA – Curb.

Lary – British slang. To be loud, aggressive, and antisocial. (Pronounced – Lair-ree.)

Old Bill/ Plods – Slang for; The police/ local law enforcement, same as Boys in Blue.

Grass/grasses – a snitch, someone who tells to police/authorities about someone's dodgy acts.

Banter – The playful and friendly exchange of teasing remarks.

Chino – A pair of trousers made from chino cloth, generally referred to as chinos.

Boot – Trunk.

Secondary school – Equitant to high school. Ages 13-17.

Clock – To see or to watch something, Cockney slang.

Flat – Apartment/condo.

Boat – Cockney rhyming slang, 'Boat Race' - Face

Bin – Waste bin, under table office bin for rubbish.

Bog– Slang for Toilet, loo, bathroom.

Shooters – Slang for guns.

* This book contains, Drama, ***Profanity and* VERY *Mature content*,** intended for readers *18+* *

Samantha Fontien

1

MADE OF

My mind is on the job. I'm known for my *focus*. I have balls of steel and ice running through my veins.

It's taken years to build up the reputation I have… I am known as the '*ultimate Hardman*', my name alone demands respect.

As I said, my mind is on the task in hand and that is sorting out a very naughty boy.

You see, he's been dipping his hand into my pockets…

Normally I wouldn't get involved in a runt like this, but examples have to be made… Lessons taught.

And today I am the mean bastard headmaster, who *runs* **this** school of life...

The cunt is on his knees, he's begging for forgiveness, for mercy.

But there ain't none. Did I say, I also show **no mercy**.

No... You don't get to where I am, showing *any* sign of weakness.

I'm numb to his pleas. I know he's crying, begging he won't do it again... I've heard it all before. So now I let my selective deafness kick in.

He's at my feet, his arms clenched tightly around my ankles pleading with me...

I look to my men. My look says it all. *I will be having words with them* later.

They pull him off me. I stand like I'm bolted to the ground, he claws in desperation, as they almost throw him into the chair.

My chair!! I'm quite proud of the chair. Like me, it has *rep too*. It should do…

We're famous, we're legends...

My chair is aptly an antique dentists chair… With a few customised modifications.

That being the steel cuffs that restrain one's arms and legs. As you can imagine, they are non obstructing for the purpose of torture, making hands and feet, just that bit easier to get to.

And so… As he screams for them not to do this, he can fix it, get me my money… I notice the fuckers blood on my shoe. He's seen it too…

It's strange, *this* brings more fear to his face. It's something more for me to work with… I could smell it from him, the moment I drove into this warehouse. I look at him, my eyes have narrowed.

"Now, look at that?" I look to my shoe and back to him. He has stopped struggling with my boys and Freddie, *'the cunt'* in question, is frozen with fear as the final cuff is snapped shut. "I do believe… I have your blood on my shoe?"

The colour from his face has completely drained now. He tries to speak, but nothing comes out…

"New shoes Freddie," I tilt my head, enhancing my sarcasm, like he should have known better. I see his eyes glaze with tears.

"You *do* know, *I like* my shoes Freddie, don't you?"

I look over at him. I don't have to over kill on the menacing, it comes natural to me. I told you... I'm a cold bastard. I tut, adding a little more adversity to the situation.

"This is quite an ominous state of affairs for you, Freddie," he is watching me like the frightened little mouse he is. "You *know* this ain't going to end good," I start to walk towards him.

I have to say, I set a scene well. I chose this place because it's an isolated warehouse, out in the docks. It's as scary as fuck.

He can scream all he wants, and *he will*, no one will hear him, hence why I like this spot.

I turn to him, I know my eyes are cold, almost black, pretty much like the 'rock I have, instead of a heart'.

Anyway, enough about me for the moment... Back to the task in hand, and that is dealing with this little cunt.

"So Freddie," I lean into him, the palms of my hands resting on my thighs.

"You've been a naughty boy," he's back to his fish impression again, lost for words. "A very naughty boy," I stare at him, immune to the puppy dog eyes he's giving me. "You must take me for a 'right *proper cunt*'?"

I step back, looking at his reactions. He's shaking his head '*NO*' frantically, the tears are popping out of his eyes, like popcorn.

"Freddie... You should have known better. You fuck with the bull... You get the horns," I look at him, before turning and walking towards the medical table.

It's a fine display, a mixture of tools and medical instruments, they all look quite nasty. I don't even look at him, as I pull on the latex gloves, I'm completely composed'...

"You know what is going to happen don't you?... *You* should have known *it,* when you had the bright idea, of dipping your *grubby fingers* into my pockets." My hand is hovering, I turn to see his eyes bulge like a Chihuahua's with pure unadulterated fear, as my hand glides over the power drill.

So power drill it is...

I pick it up and walk towards him, as I press the trigger the drill springs into action.

I rev it a few times as I walk, then I notice the puddle of water emanating out from the chair...

"Oh Freddie," I shake my head. "*Pissing yourself?*" I shake my head, while I tut again. "Seems you're good at taking the *piss*?" I look at him menacingly. "I was originally thinking of drilling your kneecaps... **However**," I press the trigger again and the drill bursts into action. "Now... I'm gonna drill... To see if you have *any balls?*"

I move towards him, the drills trigger is locked and whirring, it makes contact with him...

I feel it squelch, ripping, gnawing, as the drill bit tears through his jeans and into his flesh.

He screams like a girl, wriggling in the chair like a fish on a line. The lads restrain him as he flays around. I know the steel cuffs are cutting into him too, they have to be with all the moving he is doing.

The claret is squirting... I know I've hit a major artery with all the jerking he's doing.

Who does he think he is? *Fucking* John Travolta, in Saturday Night Fever?

There is no point in telling him not to move... You have a drill, in your nuts and let's see how much you'd move?

I'm looking him dead in the eyes. Even as the bit, hits his pelvic bones.

I feel them crunching against the metal. I know I have a snarl on my face.

No... I'm *not* enjoying it. Who would enjoy doing something like this?

But things like this, *are* necessary in my line of business.

Okay, a power drill, may be 'a tad too much' in your world... In mine... It's necessary.

Why you ask?

Simple, As I said... *You too, would piss or even shit yourself, if a power drill was aimed at you, by some nutter?*

Me? I'm traditional with my approach. I was originally going for the sledge hammer and my intentions were; *I was gonna kneecap the fucker, and maybe... Take his jaw out for six months or so, while it was wired together repairing.* But, I really couldn't help myself when I saw the look in his eyes.

See... I work on *fear*...

Fear is what makes you pay me... Respect me... For *me,* to keep an eye on things, keep trouble from *your* door.

Lets people know that *you* are under **my wing.** There are some very nasty people out there, and they *will* take advantage...

I keep the 'Lions at bay'.... **I** just happen to be '*head of the pride*'.

The fucker has passed out and is bleeding like a bitch on my chair.

I pull the drill out, as it spins, splattering the remains of *its* time spent in Freddie, on the ground, like bird shit. I calmly walk back to the table and place the drill down.

I take off my gloves and drop them down onto the table before I turn to see the lads un-cuffing a limp and 'soon to be', lifeless Freddie.

"Get that ball-less fucker out of my sight," the lads nod as they drag him across the dusty concrete floor.

I know he's not going to be a problem anymore, he never *was*...

He *was* nothing, and *now, a lesson, a warning* for the other *'little cunts'* out there, who think they are brave enough to cross me.

It's not personal, it's *business*... Unless *you* make it personal... *Then...* You *really don't* want to cross *my* path...

I look at my watch. Even I'm surprised at the time. Dealing with Freddie, took quicker than I thought. Mind you, dealing with a git like Freddie, is not really worthy of someone of my talents. But, today, I felt it was essential.

One always has to keep their blades sharp and ready.

I turn and walk towards my car. I start the engine, immediately she purrs. I pull out of the warehouse and drive through the docks. You can't beat a Jaguar for a touch of class. She screams it with her soft leather and walnut finishes. Image is everything in my game. And I mean everything.

My suits are from my tailors in Saville Row, shirts and shoes, pretty much the same. Long gone are my Fred Perry and jeans, hooligan days. I'm known now, as a man of class. Mind you some of the birds I've fucked, I would hardly call classy.

I'm on my way around to one of them right now... A *non classy* bird that is...

My cock needs to be sucked. It's the only way I can get rid of all this pent up energy I have left after dealing with Freddie so swiftly.

The drill worked better than I thought.

Mind you, having your testicles drilled, will, and can *only,* lead to your untimely and rapid demise. I'm more than familiar with anatomy, enough to know where *all* the major arteries are. I can make it quick, or make it last for days, weeks even.

I pull up in an estate, outside a block of flats, with kids swarming like rats everywhere. One day, and not in the far and distant future, at least ¾ of them, will work for me, in one way or another.

I don't have to worry about my car here. *No one* would touch it, they know it's *mine*.

Two minutes later and I am ringing the doorbell of this 'right dirty bint'.

I know she is sweet on me, can't blame her. I'm 'the man', and she knows it.

She's delighted to see me of course, I see her nipples pop at the sight of me in the tight little barely there dress she is wearing. She is always gagging for my cock and she will be.

Told ya, 'dirty bint'.

Before she says anything, I move towards her. My mouth is on hers, it's the best way to silence this bitch or she will nag or moan about this or the other.

I haven't come here as an agony aunt... I'm here to get my fuck on, and that is what I intend on doing. I back her into her sitting room, my mouth still on hers.

I pull her away from my mouth and push her onto her knees, in front of me, by her shoulders. She knows the score, as she unzips me and starts sucking on my cock.

I look down at her head bobbing forwards and backwards as she watches me.

I place my hand to the back of her head and push down, deep into the back of her throat. I feel her gagging, choking on my cock. As her eyes start to water, her throat contorts around my cock, I push harder, fucking her mouth.

She is loving it...

I pull her to me, as my cock rams down her throat. I know she wasn't ready for me, it don't stop me though. Her hands are on my thighs. I grab her hair and pull her off my cock, pulling her up to me. I look her in the eyes, they are wild with desire for me. I push her buttons.

She fucking loves it rough.

I slam her against the wall, facing it. My one hand holds her at the back of her neck firmly. I kick open her legs. My other hand moves to her thighs and under the mini dress she is wearing.

I pull her panties to the side. Grabbing my cock, I place it against her opening. I can see her trying to look at me. As she turns her head to look, I ram it hard into her, to her gasps of excitement.

I fucking love it when they do that. It's expected, I have not only length but girth too. No matter how many times I've fucked them, they all do it, like it's the first time, *every time*.

I push hard, grinding and slamming into her. She is loving it. The harder the better.

She starts to moan a series of '*Mmmmmm's*', as she finishes the last, I slowly pull out.

I place my crown against her ring, she feels it, I can feel the excitement in her build.

I push my cock hard into her arse, no lube, bitch don't need it. Told you, she likes it rough.

Its tight, which I enjoy. No matter how many times I've fucked *this arse*, it always feels tight. Her eyes are wild with lust.

As I bury my cock deeper, she cries out for '*more... To fuck her harder... Faster*'.

I oblige, I pull her tits, tweaking her nipples, as my thighs slam against her arse cheeks. It drives her nuts, like I knew it would. I know it also makes her bend over more. I like watching my cock sliding in and out of her, makes me throb in her, which only makes her '*Mmmmm*' again.

She looks back at me, she has that look in her eyes, she knows it drives me wild. I pull out of her and grab her by the hair. I walk, tugging her by the hair as I do, before throwing and bending her over the back of the sofa. She looks back at me smiling, her arms spread across the top...
She knows and *wants,* what's coming...

I don't even have to pull her cheeks apart, my cock, slides nicely back up her tight little arse.

I place my hand on her spine, my fingers trail up, towards her neck.

I grab the back of her hair again and wrap it around my fist and pull, as I ram my cock into her, pounding the fuck out of her.

And believe me, this girl can take a pounding.

I feel the cum build, she is howling, like a wolf at the moon.

She grips firmer onto the backrest as my hips slam hard into her. She is loving the pulverizing I'm giving her arse.

I'm so caught in the moment, I don't even hear myself growl.

I'm near and she knows it, enough to turn and drop to her knees as I slow and pull out of her.

She takes over now, her mouth is back on my cock...

Told ya, dirty bint, but I love it, as I shoot my load into her mouth, she can't get enough...

She wipes her lips, still looking up at me from her knees, pleased with herself.

I pop my cock back into my trousers.

"Nice one babe," I nod to her, feeling a little less pent up. "You alright for everything?" I fix myself, as she nods a *yes*. That's my cue. "Can't stop," I smile as she gets up and goes to kiss me.

Fuck that shit... I've just gone arse to mouth on her... Yeah, like that's going to happen.

"Laters babe," I throw some cash down on her TV stand, as I pass it, and I am gone...

Yeah I'm a cunt... It was a hit and run, so fucking what?

Girls like that are two a penny, if they don't respect themselves, then why should I?

I jump in my car and make my way back to my main business, my club.

It's all 'above board'... Well, most of the time and what's more, 'legal', so it keeps the Tax man off my back. It's my 'legitimate front'.

I'm a God *anywhere* in London, and in fact, the UK. But *this* place, is my main castle. My Kingdom.

It's the place to be seen in. Being a major face myself, it draws a crowd, from 'A listers', to the 'who's, who' from all the major firms.

Members only of course, we don't let any old riff raff in.

As I walk in, I'm met by Tommy. He's my number two here. A good bloke, loyal as fuck.

We used to go school together, so you can say we go back a long way. By the way, I make friends for life, how long you live it... Well that's up to you?

"Gov," he leans in. "Freddie's bird has been phoning," he gives me one of those looks.

"Tommy... You going soft, coz you fucked his sister once, fifty million years ago?" I look up at him.

You see, Tommy ain't like me. Tommy is made from decent stuff. He's married to the love of his life. Don't stop him having a few birds on the go and the odd fuck here and there. Well, when in Rome and all...

Me, I don't do that married shit stuff. I'm a wild animal, untameable, a lion. Yeah, I have a kid. Officially, I sort of live with the mother of my boy. She's a lovely girl, she's given me a son, someone to carry on my name, my legacy. She could do better than me... I know it... She knows it...

But it's me she loves... She must do as I get away with murders with her. I can't count the amount of times she has caught me in some shape or form doing something I shouldn't.

She knows the score with me, we've been together too many years. Everyone knows she's my woman and, she *is* happy with that.

Anyway, Tommy follows me to my office at the back of the club. As we walk, the staff acknowledge me.

I notice the new waitress. Hard not to, lovely pair of tits. Enough that I stop, to have a better look.

"Who's that?" I motion my head in her direction.

"Kelly," Tommy mumbles, he knows what's coming next.

"Fucking, smashing tits," I look at her, she sees me and reciprocates the moment.

However, my thoughts are of her, and that tight top slipping over her head as she's riding my cock.

Who knows, maybe she's thinking the same? The girls will do practically *anything* to get ahead in this game.

"Send her in when we've finished," I don't even take a second look at her.

He nods his agreement as we continue to my office. I settle behind my desk and watch as Tommy closes the door.

"Freddie is gone," I look at him blankly.

He nods, what else can he say or do, it's done and dusted?

He runs through what's what, and the 'goings-on' at the club. I'm listening, but at the same time, I'm looking at my phone, multitasking, that is until, something catches my eye which interests me.

These fucking social media sites, they are great for a lothario like me. It's like shooting fish in a barrel.

"What was that?" I look up at him.

"So what will I say to Freddie's bird?" He looks at me.

"*Nothing* Tommy, send her to me and I will sort it... *Story is*, he's *gone...*" I shrug my shoulders looking all innocent.

"*We* haven't a clue where *he is*? *He's* done a runner... Was fucking one of the waitresses and both of them done a sprint *sharpish*... *After* they put their hands in the till that is?" Tommy nods as my hands plea. "*Of course* he's run.. **Because**... When, *we* find him, *we* will *kill him*, *make an example* of him *won't we*?" Tommy sighs nodding. He knows the kuo. "So... Is that it?" Tommy nods again. "Good, then send that sort in, with the tits," He smiles shaking his head humourously at me.

He knows what's going to go down, and so should that girl with the tits.

And apparently she does, as I hear a 'knock' on the door...

2

EARNED IT

It's Friday night and the club is jumping. This place is always buzzing, a beautiful money earner and believe me, the money this makes... One could live like a king, which is what I do.

As I said, it's all about reputation... And that is something **I** have lots of...

You name it, I've been there, got the t-shirt. Yeah you get the picture. Whether it's business, women, places, cars, money, you name it... I've *had it all*.

... Although there are a few exceptions and I mean only a few... And one of them is in my club right now!

I saw '*Her*' the minute she walked down my sweeping staircase, looking a million dollars. Told, ya, my place is classy.

I was in my booth, surrounded by tottie. My booth has pride of place. I can see everything that's going on, from every angle.

I admit it, my cock went rock hard the minute I saw '*Her*'. Everything, the birds, the music, everything was all blurred, all expect '*Her*'...

We have history... Or rather the lack of it shall I say... Maybe it's why '*She*' has my interest?

We go way back, longer than Tommy and me. She was one of those nice pretty girls you didn't notice that much, until the tits kicked in. Yeah, that's how long I've known her.

Never made a move on her, well until it was a bit too late. See, we never seem to get the timing right. I'm blaming her too, it's not just my fault, although, I will take a shit load of it.

I'm watching her being shown to a booth, as I do, I can't help but think back to twenty odd years ago, when I thought the timing was right. Well, it was for me.

Life was different then… I was in a different class, a different league.

Back then I was a wide boy. I was given the gift of talented legs. Not only could they play amazing football, but they could run pretty fast from the 'Old Bill' too. I was always in trouble, since I was a kid and as my ole mum says *'Since I was able to walk'*.

I've always had the gift of the gab. I could and still can talk myself out of any situation, ask anyone. I have talked myself out of countless circumstances, to many to go into now, or anytime come to think of it. Let's just leave it at that.

That night I had managed to blag taking *'Her'* out for a drink down the local. Yeah, I know it sounds lame, but that's what you did in those days and under the age of twenty. Anyway, it had taken me days to get her to agree to this drink. I happened to pass where she had been working. And who knew, she worked on my doorstep. You can imagine, I was feeling pretty confident in myself. I had a pretty amazing week, as far as career advancement goes.

*Keep in mind, my idea of a career, **is** where I am, and what I do now.*

And, then to top it all off, I find out, *'She'* works on *my* doorstep... There I was, walking past an office block, minding my own business, when I see *'**Her**'*, sitting at the reception desk.

Believe me when I tell you, I had the front to walk into the building and up to that desk to chat her up. At the time, she was on a call, she knew someone was there, but not whom. That was until she finished the call and looked up, obviously flustered, trying repeatedly, to replace the handset. That's when I knew I had caught her off guard and it was finally confirmed, after years of the quick looks exchanged between both of us, that, she liked me like that.

See, you have to remember, **we** have years and years, of being around each other, but never in a romantic way, if you know what I mean.

Four days it took, going around every lunchtime, trying to break her down… Four days she resisted my charms and believe me, I laid it on thick... *I fucking wanted her… Still do.*

I look up and see *'Her'* conversing with the three Japanese business men she is seated with in the booth. She's a translator, one of the best.

She travels the world. She was always a clever girl academically, but she's not streetwise like me. We're chalk and cheese really, in that respect. *'However'*, **we are** cut from the *same cloth in so many ways, it always makes me wonder…* *Hence,* why *this*, is happening *now!!…*

And so the story continues… I meet her from work that night. I took advantage of the fact I knew she had broken up with her boyfriend. I had accidentally overheard their heated argument. She still doesn't know I was behind that wall. I heard that cunt kick off. He was lucky I was incognito, and didn't give him the pasting he deserves. *I will talk more about that prick later*. I knew when she had said yes to going for a drink that night, it was only out of spite and revenge. *See, told ya, we're cut from the same cloth.*

Being honest with ya, I was like *fuck it*, I wanted to hit that *so hard*, I would have been 'more than happy' being a rebound fuck.

Believe me, when I tell you, *'this girl'* was unnoticeable in class. *'However'*, when *'that girl'* grew tits, she became a swan.

She was, and still is the 'fabled' '*If only I ever*' * insert your preference here*.

Mine would have been at '***that*** precise moment', and I say, '*that*', because at '*that*', '*exact moment*'… It was *only* to have fucked her, to have 'had a go' on that…

What?

I'm a man, and we are talking Premier League here, not a Sunday pub footie team with beer bellies and all.

So, you get the picture of what I am dealing with here, *yeah*? Because '*this girl*', fucks with my head. Only one that could…

Well, I bring '*Her*' to my local. I wanted to 'show her off' to the boys. As I said, the girl is 'Prem League'. It would have been another string to my bow…

Little did I know… I would want to play the whole *fucking Concerto*…

So, you can imagine, I'm using my dapper charm. I know I look good, should do, my clothes always cost a small fortune, told ya, I've always liked to look good. The evening is going good, it's just her and me.

I'm trying to ply her with drinks. Which in hindsight, was a bit dopey of me, considering she had a stack of them lined up and wasn't a big drinker, still isn't.

Yeah, things you learn along the way.

I think the night is going good, she's laughing at my jokes, we talk, converse.

Yeah, that was a mistake, but you see, she is easy to talk to. She has one of those calming voices and a presence about her. That was the night I found out, '*she*' was the '*whole package*'.

There is no messing around with '*this girl*'. '*She*' is one of those '*all* or *nothing*' girls. And boy is she?

I knew it the minute I followed her into the ladies and went to kiss her. I saw it in her eyes then and still do every time I look into them, even at her pictures.

So… You're wondering, did I kiss her? Did I throw her up against the wall and devour her. If my hand slid between her legs and up that black tight mini dress she was wearing. Did I pull those panties to the side and slip my fingers in and make her cum on them, as my tongue danced in her mouth?

Did my cock get so *fucking hard* that I thought it would rip through my jeans to get to '*Her*'?

I feel my cock getting hard as I continue to watch her, remembering that night so many years ago…

No and yes, and unfortunately it's in that order.

I look down to my hard cock pitching a tent in my trousers. My justification, I do have a blonde bint stroking my thigh, but I can tell you now, it's not the bint that has my cock this hard.

Yep, and it all boils down to that one night, twenty plus years ago, in my local…

So, we're back to the ladies toilet of my local… *Yeah*, not the most romantic of places, and unfortunately, I made it *ours*. I know this as she keeps on reminding me of it. I told you, we have history.

I've leaned in for a kiss, gone for gold, no way *she* would or could resist my charms. I laugh thinking of this, as this is *me* I am talking about. You see, *this* will be a common pattern for the story of me and '*Her*'

So, I lean in…. And… She pulls back?

Yeah? This still shocks me too…

I'm standing there, thinking *'what the fuck? She's knocking 'me', back?*

Me?'

Yeah, I still *feel it* to this day. I'm *not* a man that was ever used to getting knocked back as you can imagine…

"Don't," she looks away, breaking that intense moment we are having.

I admit it, I'm a bit crushed. Undeterred, I go in again. My body moves closer to hers. I'm smooth, I can see the hairs tingling on her skin to my touch. Now, *I know,* she fucking likes me. I also know at this time, I'm not getting a quick bunk-up in the bogs.

I'm a stupid cunt to even think it in the first place, but in my defence, that is typical me, you see, I'm a Chancer… I see a chance, I take it. I'm still a man that makes things happen.

My lips are close to hers, I can feel the heat of her breath against my skin. And now, as I press my body close to hers, she can now feel my rock hard length. See, told you I was a Chancer.

"Don't," she looks at me, flashing them blue eyes of hers again.

I am holding her chin, ready to taste her lips. But I feel her slightly pull away from me.

"Why?" *This I have to know*. "You and that fucking pratt have broken up?" I know I can say this safely, as she did mention it in conversation earlier on.
"Because I don't trust myself with you?"

She looks me in the eye, and I mean dead in the eye. We are having a moment, this connection thing you hear people talking about.

"And what's wrong with that?" I smile as I go in again, all smooth like.

"Because I'm not like that?" She looks me in the eyes again. "You're mad to think what you're thinking… I'm *not* someone you'd *fuck* in the toilets?" She looks at me in disgust, quite rightly. I agree with her one hundred percent, still do.

"Then let's go outside then?" I laughed as I go in again.

Yes, in hindsight, I would have handled things very differently.

But, as '*She*' constantly reminds me, 'I don't own a time machine'. One day? Who knows, I might?

I remember her shaking her head, disappointed at me, only saying my surname. Since we have been kids, we have **never** called each other by our first names.

Only when there is something wrong, we both do it? *It's our thing.*

I must admit, I'm disappointed in me... But... And this is, what makes the messy, fucked up situation *of*, '*Her*' and me.

So, you're wondering, what happened? Why didn't I just give it all the patter, tell her what she wanted to know and get some?

That is a question I ask myself quite regularly...

One thing you need to know about me, is I don't lie. I deal with the truth, you may not like it, but that's me.

So, the truth of why I walked her home and didn't even get so much as a snog?

Because I looked into her eyes, and I saw her soul…

Like me, she is damaged by her past, we have and share complicated stories.

We are used to living with, and keeping secrets. **We are**, as I said, cut from the same cloth.

But I will say, I fell into those eyes and have somehow, never been able to climb out of them.

This I know through time…

We have crossed each other's paths too many times. Always in the same places, just with different people. It's like the God's of destiny are fucking with us? Or are they just fucking with me? Because I am a very *bad* man?

I knew what she was saying that night in the pub toilets. I heard and saw it loud and clear. Let me explain something to you. As I said earlier, like when I told you about my dirty bint?

Well, you wouldn't bring her home would you? She's a fuck and run? Night I met her, I was fucking her arse in the clubs toilets. *Yeah, seems I have a thing for that.* But I like being spontaneous, I'm a thrill seeker, an adrenaline junkie.

'*Her*', well as I said Prem league, the kind of girl you bring home, proudly to your mum, marry and knock out some very beautiful rugrats. She is someone to grow old with...

Now do you get it?

I didn't go in for the attack, because, it could have been me introducing her to the proud parents. I couldn't let that happen? I was gonna *be* somebody, I was going to run London and that wasn't on the agenda for her.

She is not like me, in the respect of she is a proper law abiding citizen. She is the two point three kids and house in the suburbs. The high flying city career. She's the kind of girl that would make you want to work hard and do well. You know that saying; 'Behind every great man... There's an even greater woman?'

Yeah...

Well, she *is that woman!!*

It was me that wasn't ready for her.

I'm not the kind of guy who does normal; my office, working hours, things in general, nothing in my life is 'normal'.

But, it was *me*. I knew I couldn't do it... Oh don't get me wrong...

I want her, always have. I just want to cut my own path. And this is what I know.

She couldn't live my life.

I tell her about it, but she doesn't want to know about anything or how I achieved my empire... She wants no part in it at all.

That kills me when I hear her say it. I think of the power couple we could be. We could run the world.

My world would love her, adore her.

She is a lady, has class, sophistication, taste. I look over at the array of bints squeezed into my booth, trying to be seen in my company. They are dressed in their cheap 'knock off' dresses, that leave very little to the imagination. It's like a uniform they all wear, so cunts like me can fuck them wherever, however and as often as we want.

My eyes quickly focus back to '*her*'. Its torture, knowing I'm in the same room as her. I feel my cock tighten again, against the fabric of my suit trousers.

I just can't sit here and do *nothing*. I have an idea.

I raise my finger to Tommy, who is standing by the bar ,to come over. He does and I whisper my idea into his ear…

3

CAN'T FEEL MY FACE

My eyes quickly focus back to *'her'*. *As I said,* Its torture, knowing I'm in the same room as her and I'm not with her.

It's been like this for more years than I care to remember...

I see the 'gorgeous Nina, one of the waitresses head to their table with a magnum of champagne, which is being held by an entourage of lap dancers behind her. I watch the Japanese guests faces light up, as Nina explains in fluent Japanese, *'Compliments of the house'*.

I see as their faces beam with delight, as the gaggle of girls swarm the booth, descending on them.

Now all I have to do is wait…

And thankfully, due to my forward thinking, my plan works. And, in no time, I see *'Her'* being nudged out of the booth, with the lack of space due to the endless line of girls, trying to 'make friends' with the Japanese guests.

See, told ya… I make things happen.

I see her arse perched on the end of the booth. My girls are good, even if I say so myself. They'll *all* earn the bonus's, I'll put in their pay-packets tonight, for sure. And knowing one or two of them the way I do, they'll also be getting paid handsomely by our *very happy Japanese gentlemen* too.

So I watch, knowing her the way I do…

I observe her give up on trying to remain seated. I notice her standing there. I also know she has zero patience. *Now*, I see she's thinking. *See*, that's one of *'Her'* problems. She over thinks things…

Something she has done since I've known her, and, to a certain extent she is actually, scarily accurate in fact, with her conclusions.

But, that's beside the point.

I always tell her, 'Life is for the living'... And *'She'* should start doing it, living that is'. And, it's the very reason, *'She'* is here tonight... Her work that is, when she told me her idea, I told her to go for it. I even offered to throw some money her way, you know, finance it. But, being who and how she is, she wouldn't hear nothing of it. Point blank refusing every time. And she even knows when I've sent work her way. It's like she smells it's me, or something. She's too proud. Another thing we have in common... Pride. We are both as 'stubborn as mules', and will be more than happy, 'to cut off our own noses, to spite our faces'... Hence, the *mess* that is *'us'*?

I can see she is getting antsy now. She is defo not going to be having anymore of this behaviour from the dancers. 'She' looks highly unimpressed, as she watches the girls literally shove and wiggle their tits into the men's faces.

Now should be a good time for me to step in. *This should be good.*

"Oi, oi," I walk towards her. I know she's heard me, even above the music, which is thundering out.

She turns, the look on her face of course is of surprise. But I also know she is pleased to see me.

"I'm not even going to ask," she shakes her head in disbelief. She looks around.

"I should have known *you'd* be here," her eyes flash at me as she rolls them.

She then, motions in the direction of one of the girls, who is *literally* jiggling her tits in one of the men's faces and he is loving *every min*ute of them DD's.

"I could be offended if I didn't know what you meant," I laugh at her.

"*Why*? You were *meant to be*," she smiles knowingly at me. *I fucking love her sass.*

"And *you've* started *already*?" I look at her amused.

I'm giving her, one of my knowing looks.

"Looks like my work for the night is done," she smiles motioning over to the booth, as she clutches her drink, which knowing her, is just a full fat coke.

"Surely you knew you wouldn't be in here long?" I know she is looking at me puzzled now. *You see,* we play a cat and mouse game. *So*, I continue to taunt her. "Well, most of these places nowadays, have *translators but ones* who *can* actually *dance*?" I raise my eyebrows like I am as clever as fuck.

I am actually, it's *my* idea, I'm the one that started that gig in the clubs. Keeps all the money in-house, plus they tip better, spend more.

"*Ooh*," I see, she makes sense of the situation and the lack of space for her in the booth. "I suppose I'd better go then?"

Err no, that's not how this is going down… The Chancer kicks in.

"I have a booth, come over and have a drink with me? I know there's loads of space for you there," I look sincere, of course I do, it's my club after all. I motion over to it. "Just one drink?" I wink at her.

I see that '*She's*' doing that 'over thinking thing', again.

"Come on, park your arse, even for just five minutes," I look at her innocently . "One drink?" She looks at me, I know I have her on the fence. "It's *only a drink?*" I look at her one last time with a smirk, before I take the drink out of her hand and walk over to my booth, leaving her with no choice, but to follow me.

"*A drink?* That's how *all* of this started," she laughs shaking her head, as she follows me.

Everyone knows the kuo in a situation like this… And that is… *Keep the fuck away from my booth and don't cock block me.*

I'm being a good boy, when really I want to just lean over and devour her.

"So how long are you here for this time?" I sip casually on my scotch. "Actually… How comes you didn't tell me you were coming?" I give her one of my looks.

"Which one do you want me to answer?" *See,* this is why she gets my cock so fucking hard.

"Both questions," I laugh, I love her dry wit.

"Which first?" Her eyebrows are raised. She is clearly taking the preverbal.

I look at her, she is stifling the big smile she is concealing. She knows, she is winding me up and she is loving every minute of it, as usual.

"Okay," she throws her eyes up to the heavens, as though the jig is up. "I've been here for a week." I go to interrupt, but she gives me one of those '*shut the fuck up looks*', I know, as I have given enough of them to know one. "And, because *I knew*, **you** would be busy," she shrugs nonchalantly.

"Bullshit," I call her out.

"Bullshit?" She looks at me questionably.

"*Yeah…* Bullshit," I call her out on it again.

"Why bullshit, when I told you the truth?"

Now I have annoyed her. That's actually not a hard thing for me to do. I seem to have a natural talent in upsetting her. I tend to quite often. in some shape or form. And she is right, we do the truth thing one-hundred percent with each other.

"You know I am *never* busy for you?" She knows I am offended. " *So...* Bullshit answer," I look at her miffed.

"Not fair, you know you've been busy when I've been here before?" She looks pleadingly at me. And I know she needs me to acknowledge the truth of her statement.

"That's different," I look solidly at her. "I couldn't."

"*I know,*" she looks into her drink. And she does know.

There have been things going on, things I can't and won't go into now. But, they needed dealing with. Again, she knows all this.

"So, how long left?" I try to break the uncomfortable silence.

"I'm leaving the day after tomorrow," she looks over in the direction of her clients booth, which is still heaving with tits and teeth.

"So soon?" I try and hide the disappointment in my voice.

See, this is our problem, *timing*. We can't get our planets aligned, or whatever they say.

"Yes, afraid so," she reaches for her drink.

I'm not going to waste anytime in playing fifty questions. The one thing I have learned in my forty plus years is… *Time is precious*. We waste so much.

"You staying at Emma's?" She nods 'yes'. "Come on… I'll give you a lift," I get up and she follows me towards the exit of the club.

As I lead the way, I turn around, to see her stop.
"What's up?" I ask, *fuck*, she is having seconds thoughts. *See*, I mentioned she does this over thinking thing didn't I?

"I need to tell them I am going?" She looks over in their direction.

"They're big boys, I'm sure they will figure that out themselves," I laugh.

"It's not good manners," she looks at me. "In Japanese culture, manners and respect are everything."

I get that with the Japanese, they have a great mythology. I also know, bad manners are a complete no, no with her too. *See*, this 'years' of knowing someone.

"I'll get a message to them," I shrug my shoulders, at the simplicity of the solution. "Them men are busy," I laugh.

"*Errm*, no you can't?" She looks at me and I'm thinking what the *fuck now*? All I want to do is get out of this fucking place. "Won't the owners be miffed at you doing something like that?"

Bless her and her innocence of situations like this. See, not streetwise.

"*Errm*… I think I can," I laugh, mimicking her, as I grab her arm and walk her out. "*It's my club*," she stops trying to un-hook my grip of her as she protests and starts to walk with me, stunned with my answer.

See, she's not the only one who hasn't told each other about recent events or circumstances.

I walk her out of my club and towards my car.

'*She*' turns to look at me as I press the button on the fob and the doors unlock instantly.

I'm giving it my best gentlemanly behaviour. I watch her lean against the door. Her arms are folded.

So, that means, one, she is hostile and, two… An arms folded pose, clearly says *fuck off I'm not having your shit*. She is looking right through me, like she does. She knows me too well. And I mean too well. She knows things about me I haven't discovered for myself.

I fight the temptation of just leaning in for a kiss. This is not going to be another toilet situation down at the local.

The atmosphere is electric between us.

It is anytime we make contact, and it doesn't matter by what medium either. We ignite each other's flames, fires, whatever.

You'd think we'd stop playing around and just do something. But we are cautious and I mean *'both of us'*.

I know she will be a raging inferno, and I will be engulfed…

I know I will be scarred for life, I already am by her. It will be all consuming, and that fucking excites me.

For '*Her*'? My worry is that she would be engulfed in the flames of my world, in one way or another.

I haven't led a very good, clean life. One day... I know there will have to be some form of 'retribution' for what I have done.

Whether it is on this earth or another, I know that day will come, I will be judged... I just don't want her suffering for my sins too.

So, now I'm feeling like how I did all those years ago in the bogs of my local.

Do I or don't I?

I don't have time to second guess myself, when I feel her soft lips brush against mine.

Her mouth is hungrily on mine. I reciprocate her advances. I take her into my arms feeling her nestle against my body.

I am rock hard, and she can feel it. I was hard from the moment I saw '*Her*'. Only '*She*' makes me like that, no one else. I even have to think of her, at times, just to get hard, when the need arises. *And* she knows all about this *too*.

'*She*' knows how to push my buttons. The countless typed conversations we've had, that have left me *very* blue balled.

I've knocked a good few out to those and to her phone calls, too. We jump from subject to subject, we can talk about anything and often do. I've told her things I've told no other. She's also clever enough to read between the lines on some of the things I have told her. She gets me like no other. See, this is the history bit thing we have.

My tongue is dancing with hers. I have her still pressed up against the door of the Jaguar. I am devouring her. Consumed totally, I have thought about doing *exactly this* for too many years, far too many not to be experiencing what I am feeling right now.

I am on fire... I am for the first time 'alive.'.. I can feel my heart racing and banging at the same time. I can feel the blood coursing around my body.

I've tried most of the drugs out there, and nothing compares to the *rush* I am experiencing at this moment.

I wanted to kiss her slowly, tease her with my tongue, but the lion in me is roaring. It normally does with any contact I have with her... But this??

This is something else, she is finally in my arms, I am like a savage devouring her mouth.

My hands want to explore her, rip at her clothes, but I am surprisingly controlled considering. I haven't even touched her breasts yet. I find myself going into gentleman mode.

That's when I'm saved by the bell, literally as it shakes me out of my lustful fantasy...

I answer it, seeing it is Tommy. I listen to him, giving her '*I'm sorry for the interruption*' look. She watches me and I her, I see her face drop slightly. It's like she can hear what Tommy is saying in my ear. Or, knowing her, she's seen the look on my face. I hang up and turn to her.

"Yeah, yeah," she shakes her head. "I should have known," she laughs.

See, it's like she has a sixth sense...

"I'm sorry... It should only take a few minutes?" I look to her. Reality is, I should have known better. I knew this situation would take longer. "What about if I call you later?" I know I am chancing my luck big-time.

"No," she laughs. "You're okay," and now she is giving me one of those 'You've totally blown it' looks.

Now... I'm in a dilemma...

There are urgent matters that need my attendance in the club... Or, do I do, what I want to do and take her to a hotel?

I know which one I want to do...

But, you don't get to my position, doing things you want to do...

I look at her, she is still looking at me, but there is '*that* look'. One I have avoided for a very long time. I know I have disappointed her over the years, but I've managed to dodge the actual face to face look.

As I said, we share lots of traits, lots of life similarities... Except, we handle things differently.
We both deal with things head on, just in our own ways, mine are just, well, let's just say, if you're seeing my eyes, you're in big trouble.

These are not eyes you can stare into for very long without feeling the ice cold that blazes through them... That's when of course '*She*' isn't around.

"Let me call you a taxi?" There's no point in arguing, what's done is done.

"Yes, do," she looks up at me, it's one that cuts like a knife.

Typical, a black cab has just dropped of a punter. She has her hand raised to alert the driver, just in time for him to switch back off his light with a smile on his face.

Yeah fucker, it's not everyday he'd have a sort like this in his cab. I walk with her and open the door. I don't want her to go, but duty calls. I go to lean in to peck her on the cheek. But she turns and steps into the cab and sits in the back seat. I have no choice, but to close the door. My eyes are on her, she staring straight ahead, ignoring me. She knows that winds me up. I move to the drivers passenger window. He drops the window.

"Yes, Gov?" His eyes are wide with fear. He has recognised me.

"Take the lady to wherever she needs to go," I look at him, handing him a wad of money.

He nods, and pulls out onto the London road and they are gone. *Now I am fucked off royally.*

I let the anger engulf me as I march up the few steps to the club and in through the doors.

I make my way through the club and towards my office out the back.

As I get to the hallway, I can hear a familiar voice. Without hesitation I make my way into the office.

Tommy is standing at the foot of my desk. In the chair in front of him is Tracie, one of my sorts. She would be one of my favourites, out of the harem that I hold.

I walk to my desk, as I do Tracie looks up at me. I can see the huge black eye and bust lip she has. I grab her chin gently and look at her.

"He was kicking the door in demanding to see Africa," her eyes quickly look to the floor as I examine her face. "I was worried about someone calling the police, he was making a lot of noise," she looks to the floor again. "So I let him in."

She knows she made the wrong choice, well, as for her ex, he is a proper wrong-un.

"Why didn't you phone me ?" I look at her, she knows the score, she knows better than this.

She can't even look at me. Yeah, she has made countless bad choices.

"Where's the baby?" I look to her.

Africa, the kid, is not mine, but she's a lovely little thing. Believe it or not, I like kids and they me.

I believe in kids being kids for as long as they can, but sometimes, life makes you grow up quicker than you should.

"She's round at Cathy's, my neighbour," she looks glumly at me.

I know what has to be done. I look to Tommy, who just blinks his eyes the once. He knows the score. He steps forward.

"Here Tracie, let's get you home love," he places his hand on her arm.

She gets up and starts to walk with him, looking behind at me as he guides her gently out the door.

Before the door is even closed I'm on my mobile, a few calls have to be made...

4

MAKE IT RAIN

Now, you're possibly thinking I'm fucking nuts for blowing '*Her*' out for Tracie?

Yes, I am in a way... However, her ex is being a disrespectful little fucker. He knows she is with *me*. He knew what he was doing when he knocked at her door. He knew he was bringing Armageddon into his life fucking with me. I gave him enough warnings before.

In less than five minutes my Range Rover pulls up outside the backdoor. I stroll down the steps to the awaiting vehicle. The door opens, I step in and we drive off.

Soon enough we are at a small estate. Mickey Rice put the word out on the street. Funny, when certain people put the feelers out, what news comes in and how quick.

From the information that has been obtained. He only got home less than three minutes ago. There are four very burly, thug looking men who get out of the Range Rover and one of them is me. We have baseball bats, with the exception of Mickey, who has a bowling bag full of nasty tools. We make our way into the four story block. We know exactly where we are going. It's very helpful that the cunt has turned on his music and the thumping of his base speakers will do very nicely in muffling any screams that will emanate from his flat.

I know this estate well, I have a few dealers who operate here for me. *In fact*, it was one of them, who grassed on this shithead's, being back on the estate.

We are at his door, Mickey gives it a wrap with his knuckles. We are all surprised to hear the door open as we look between ourselves. We were expecting to have had to kick the door in. How that fuckwit ever heard us above the noise, God only knows.

But anyway, it's too late, as Mickey is through the door before the fucker even has a chance to react. The lads push through as he struggles and tries to flee…

I walk calmly through the door. I think he thought he was just getting turned over, that was, up until he saw *ME*. His face says it all… Pure utter *FEAR!!*

He tries to make a run for it, breaking free and running with all his might… But the lads are too quick, they stop him jumping off his second floor balcony, to his freedom. My lads are too on the ball, and after a small scuffle they drag him back as he kicks and pleads. They throw him onto his knees in front of me. I say nothing as I stare down at him, slowly shaking my head menacingly.

Yeah, he's already started begging as expected… I'm not even going to waste my time listening to this cunt's plea's, as he shakes like a leaf.

I am silent, as I lift the baseball bat into the air, I look the cunt in the eye, as I swing...

I hear it crack and ricochet against his skull, the claret sprays everywhere. I swing again and again, the thud of the bat vibrates up my arm, nevertheless, I swing once more.

In no time, the fucker is cataleptic on the floor, in a foetal position.

I step back, the bat hanging limply at my side. I can hear the thumps of the lads bats making contact with him.

I hear him whimpering through the thuds and the sound of metal and wood, smashing against his bones.

It's only when he stops moving, that '*they stop*' and the bats finally become motionless.

Poor fucker is making gurgling noises now, I hear the swish of a bat through the air and an almighty sickening thud. The bat has split what's left of this cunts face open. He is lucky he got the bats and that I didn't take a blade from Mickey's bag and open him up like the little runt he is.

The men look to me, I nod enough and they back off him. The three of them stand over him, observing his movement if any. If he does, there will be another few clumps to be had, until the job is done.

He is barely breathing, but that is *only* because the cunt is, 'Africa's father'.

He's never paid a penny in maintenance for her, that comes down to me too, all out of *my* pocket.

I'm the one that bungs Tracie the money so she can feed the baby, put nappies on her and have a few nice treats, *not him*. I even pay her rent.

Cunt has had it coming for a while. From what I understand, he is back from taking a year out?

How someone can decide to take a fucking year out of a kids life, because they want to *find* themselves? And then breeze back in like nothing has happened, is beyond me?

Nothing is said as we all walk back to the Range Rover and pile in. He's not a popular fella anyway, I'm sure the old Bill, will put two and two together and think it is a drug deal gone wrong.

I call Tommy and arrange to have my car dropped off at Steph's. She would be the top princess of my harem. She knows the kuo and is more than delighted to see me. She never asks too many questions.

She's on me like a rash,, its been a couple of weeks since I've seen her and she wants my cock like she's a sex starved whore.

The doors not even closed when she is stroking my cock and trying to shove her tongue down my throat.

Normally I would be more than happy to oblige, but I have that cunts blood all over me. Fucker sprayed blood, like a fountain. If we'd be stopped by the plods I would have definitely got nicked.

I head upstairs and into the bathroom with her following me.

She undresses me and herself, smothering me with kisses. Normally I would be fucking her in the shower by now. But all I can think about is *'Her'* face when I took Tracie's call.

Steph's hands are on my cock and balls, as she guides me back into the walk-in shower. She turns the water on and it cascades over us. The remnants of the cunts blood, mixes with the water and washes down the drain.

Steph looks at me, my cock isn't hard. I think of *'Her'* and it starts to stir. I think of *'Her'* mouth on mine. *'Her'* tongue, the feel of *'Her'* hot wet tongue, sliding with mine.

My cock springs to attention. *Yeah*, I'm a complete bollocks thinking of *'her'* to get myself hard for another woman, but duties must, and all.

Now Steph is a nice girl, a raving sort as far as sorts go. She is mine, until I don't want her. I look after her needs and she looks after mine.

It's a great set up for us both. But she knows, when I call, she is to be ready for me.

I knew straight away when I started seeing her that she was up for anything and that she would become one of my favourites. And she is pretty much up for anything. She likes to call herself *'experimental'*. I just think she likes to get her freak on and I'm game with that.

"Mmmmmmm, your cock is so big and hard," she moans as she presses her soapy tits against me. "I need it in me."

Her fingers glide over me as she drops slowly to her knees. I'm still thinking of *'Her'*, thinking its *'Her'* fingers against my skin.

And *BINGO, I am rock hard*, my cock is in Steph's mouth as she moves her lips up and down on my shaft. I watch her, my fingers trailing over her chin. The water drips off us. I watch, as she takes my cock further each time she descends until I am deep in her throat.

I reach my hand down to her extended throat and feel my cock moving through it.

I can feel the snarl on my face, my animal instincts surge in and I push my cock deeper as she, looks up at me, with them big doe eyes like a porn star.

I dip my cock further, nudging, pushing a little more.

I can see she is turning red with lack of air, so I pull out from the depths of her throat until her lips are once again around my crown.

"Stand against the wall," I growl at her.

She obeys and I move towards her, my mouth claims hers. I reach for her tits and pinch on her nipples. I twist them, rolling them with just enough pressure to make her gasp and eyes narrow.

Her hand reaches down to my cock and she pulls it towards her. I grab her leg, lifting it up and she immediately places my cock at her opening.

"*Fuck me*," she breaths hard, her eyes narrow.

I push my cock hard into her as she gasps and start to fuck her, pushing her up against the tiled wall. My hips slam into her, I pull her into me, my rhythm, a perfect motion as I ram my length into her inner core. She bites her lip stifling her cuming "*Mmmmmm's*" and she is cuming hard.

I slow, teasing her sweet tight pussy as she cums on my cock, her juices gather on the base of my rod.

But I still fuck her, grinding my hips and tip deep in her until she is singing '*Ohh God,*' as I hit that spot repeatedly.

Her skin is electric to my touch, her nipples are hard, begging for my teeth, so I oblige. Her nipple is trapped between my teeth with just enough pressure, my tongue teasing. I feel her pussy tighten around my shaft, as she cums again. As her pussy bounces on my cock, I suck her tits hard, as I ram my cock faster, harder...

I'm going to cum. My mouth moves to her neck and I fuck her faster, she is bouncing vigorously as I slam firmly, the cum is rising...

Her mouth is on mine when I pump my load deep into her. She is gasping for breath and looking into my eyes like she has won the lottery. I suppose she has in a way. It's a good hard fuck.

"That's one for the books," she breaths like she is 'high on love', which I know she is.

She has cum, like a devil on heat and is all loved up. She would call what we done *'making love'*.

Me, good, 'hot fucking', even if I do say so myself.

See, this is why I haven't seen her for a couple of weeks. She is getting too attached, so I backed off.

She needs to get used to me not being around if she wants to go down that road. She knows it's one '**I don't walk**'.

She knew the score when I started seeing her. I told her the kuo and she was all up for it. But *they* always change. They *all* start off with good intentions, thinking they can handle it, me, and what I offer... *And most do for a while...*

Well it's a good thing innit, they *are* onto a good thing with me. I help them out, pay bills, sort out any problems they may have. But I don't do strings, well only the ones on my own bow.

Now, you *see*, I'm thinking of '*her*' again. *Everything* it seems, boils down to '*Her*'...

I dry off and walk into the bedroom and get into bed. I watch as Steph picks up my clothes and deals with them. She don't batter an eyelid to the claret that is on it. She even says she's going to soak my shirt with some of that cleaning product from the telly. I say nothing as I flick on the TV and wait for her to come back up. Which she does armed with food.

See, she's a clever girl, knows the way to a man's heart is through his stomach. Shame I don't have a heart.

I'm always hungry after I have dealt with business, that and sex, so I am ravenous as you can imagine having done both. I finish the food and fuck Steph again, even drilling her arse.

The morning arrives and I am pitching a tent. Steph is stirring, so I give her a nudge with my cock. Nothing like a bit of morning glory. She is more than happy to slip under the covers and starts giving me a nosh.

Before I know it, she pulls back the covers and crawls above me, her legs either side of me.

She sits just below my balls, and brings the palm of her hand to her mouth. She licks her fingers like a dirty slut and places them down at her clit. Her fingers swirl around it and I see her pussy start to soften as she smiles minx like. "*Mmmmm*," she moans as she slips in a finger, followed by another.

My cock thumps as I watch her dip her fingers in and out of her before she kneels up and takes hold of my cock.

With a deviant smile she slips my cock into her as she slides down it. Her fingers dip into my mouth and I taste her. She runs one over my lips and leans over.

Her tongue brushes over them, licking her pussy cream from me, before she starts to devour me as she rides me like a cowgirl.

She leans back, taking my full length as I watch it slide in and out of her. I grab her hips, pulling her back and forth. Great thing about Steph is, that she can cum on command, she is a cum machine. She's a noisy sort too, loves talking dirty when she's being fucked, and this morning is no different.

"I'm gonna cum on your cock again baby, *Mmmmm*," she moans. "Come on, make me cum again on that big fat cock of yours," she moans licking her lips seductively.

I pull her hips harder, faster, jolting her back and forth on my length as she takes it all.

"That's it baby, make me cum," she snarls as she starts to pull on her nipples. "Fuck my wet pussy... Mmmmm, that's it… Bury your cock deep in my cunt."

She moves like she is making for the finishing line.
She wants me to spank her to bring her over the edge, so I slap her arse.

My hand is numb as I slap her it harder and harder as she pushes into my cock.

I thrust '*it*' into her, harder, faster as she bounces against me.

I'm fucking her like a jackhammer when she begs for me to '*fuck her harder, she is cuming*'.

My heart races like I'm a Kenyon marathon runner, as I fuck her as fast as I can. I kneel up and lay her down on the mattress. I'm holding her hips as I gyrate hard into her, watching my cock move in and out of her wet pussy. She's pulling on her nipples again as I grind hard into her.

She's dragging her bottom lip through her teeth, she is on fire as she tells me to choke her hard. My hand reaches down to her throat and I squeeze on it.

Her faces lights up as I tighten my grip with every ram my cock makes up her. I can feel her pussy tighten around my cock.

I squeeze harder, slamming my length in and out of her.

I move faster, as I feel her pussy tighten again and a rush of her cum on my cock. I lean over and whisper in her ear.

"I'm gonna cum as I choke the fuck out of you," I growl as my teeth nibble at her ear as she revels in it.

My hand tightens its grip more, as I fuck her as hard as I can. She pulls me into her grabbing my arse, as I feel the cum rise.

My animal instincts go into overdrive as I pump my cum deep into her, smashing into her with my hips. All I hear is the slaps of our skin, I fuck her, sliding in and out of her slowly until the last drop is in her and release my grip on her throat. My energy is depleted.

I roll off her and lie on my back, comfortably numb as she rolls onto my chest. Her hand strokes and teases my abs.

I lie there for ten minutes before I get up and head into the shower. Steph goes to join me, but I'll be here all day if she has her way, and I have things to do...

So I tell her not now with a simple look.

After my shower I get dressed and go downstairs for breakfast.

See, I have clothes here for events like this. To me they are not only alibis, they are safe houses too.

Steph knew the score when she wasn't invited into the shower.

It's probably why she has a face like a wet weekend, she serves me up bacon and eggs.

"So what time?" She is asking what time I *allegedly* got here.

"Eleven o'clock," I continue to eat.

She says nothing as she nurses her cup of coffee. She knows I like to eat in silence.

See, I don't get much peace or time to myself as you can imagine, so for me I have certain times when you cannot disturb me.

1.   Is when I am eating.

The other is when I am in the toilet and I don't mean at a urinal, many a business meeting has been conducted at one, as you can imagine. However, this brings me to when I am in a cubical, *at neve*r **any point** should a man be disturbed while he is having a shit...

I mean come on?

Can one simply not, shit in peace?

"You not eating?" I ask. I know it's a silly question, as judging by her weight she's been hitting the coke hard.

We all have crutches, we are all damaged in one way or another.

We all need something to lean on.

"Come, sit down and eat with me," I beckon her over.

I watch as her face light up as she pulls the chair next to mine and sits down still nursing her cup of coffee. I lift a forkful of eggs to her, but she shakes her head no.

She reaches for my hand, placing hers on it like we are playing happy fucking families.

I take a good look at her, her face is sunken, too sunken for two weeks since I last saw her. I look at her, my eyes look right through hers. It's an intimidation tactic I've perfected over the years.

She shifts uncomfortably in her seat. I know she is hiding something, so I keep my focus on her.

"How much are you shoving up your nose?" I look at her sternly. "What? You think I wouldn't know? *You're* forgetting *who* you are dealing with!!"

She looks at me, open mouthed. I reach for her hand, I need to be clever here, it is after all, the reason why I am here.

"Babe, your figure?" I look at her. "You know I love ya tits," she smiles, going all girly on me. "Don't lose your tits babe... I'd miss em," I wink at her. "You need to look after yourself."

I look at her and touch her hand to reassure her. *See* that is the chancer in me, always going for it.

I need to keep her sweet. I can't help but stare at my phone on the table.

You got it... I'm thinking of '*her*'.

Yeah, I'm calling myself a prized cunt for it.

Imagine, something you have wanted, craved even, for so long... And, for it to be snatched out of your hands.

Ok that bit is my own doing, I had a choice to make and I made it. I can't change the past.

I reach for my phone and lean down kissing her on the top of her head. Telling her I will call her later, I am out the door and walking to my car.

Oh you're wondering about where are my keys? In the car of course. And that would be the car that Tommy arranged to have brought round here last night. And, remember, this is *MY* car, no one would ever have the balls to go near it.

I start her up and I'm gone. Being all legal and that, I slide the phone into the Bluetooth thing. Yeah, you've guessed it… I'm calling '*Her*'.

See, she is like a drug. I know I'm not suppose to go there…

But I want it… And I have wanted it for too long… I am lost, consumed by it.

What I failed to tell you, is that while I was banging Steph, I was thinking of '*her*'.
She has crawled into my brain and has taken up, permanent residence there.
I've already called a few times already. I know she won't call me back, she never does.

It's always me that does the hunting or the chasing, whatever.

She knows I'll keep calling until she answers.

I know she is pissed at me for last night.

Being the brain she is, she will have put two and two together and thought it was business related.

Well it was… I had warned that little cunt twice before and that is something. And that was only because I made a promise to Tracie, he is the baby's dad after all.

But he got what he deserved, he brought disrespect to a new level doing what he did, hence his retribution being what it was.

No one is going to miss him anyway…

And to think… Out of all *his* dad's sperm, '*he*' was the strongest swimmer?

5

THE HILLS

I'm getting more fucked-off by the second, wondering how long '*She*' is going to fuck me about before picking up my call…

I pull up at a set of traffic lights and there '*She*' is, crossing the road.

'*Fuck me*'… Would you believe it?

Yeah, I know, *fucking unreal*. There '*She*' is, right in front of me.

I beep the horn and watch as she jumps almost six-foot into the air in shock, unaware of who the offending beeper is.

I observe as she stops and dips her designer shades down her nose exposing those blue eyes, peering over the shades with laser-like stare, until she sees *me*, hands on the wheel giving her a saucy wink.

'*She*' stands there, unconvinced that it is, in fact me, right in front of her. She's as shocked to see me as I her.

I motion with my head that I'll pull over and I draw up to the kerb, watching her walk up to the car in the rear view mirror.

As she approaches I push one of the buttons on the console and the passenger window descends in time for her to lean down.

"Your phone broken?" I jest with her.

"Dunno… Haven't looked at it," she looks at me nonchalantly.

But I know she is staring right through me, even though I can't see her eyes through the mirrored lenses.

"Wanna lift?" I match her coolness.

"No, I'm okay thanks," she smiles at me. "How come you're around here?"

Now, of course, I'm not going to say 'I've been fucking a bird for an alibi, am I?'

"Just sorting out some business," I laugh.

Now, I have to play it cool, remember I told you, '*She'* has a sixth sense for shit like this. She looks at me, right through me again, pursing her lips together.

There is distain on her face and, yes, it's all for *little ole me.*

"*Hmmmmm*," she purrs pondering my words.

I feel my cock stir, imagining her purring a '*Mmmmm'* instead. *Yeah* I know, I'm twisted, but as I've said ,she fucks with my head. I know she is restless so I prolong the time with her for my own amusement.

"So Emma lives round here then?" I look at her dead in the eyes.

She has never told me exactly where Emma lives, just area wise, so let's see how she will answer this in her delicate way. I watch her slide the sunglasses down her nose, just enough that I can see her eyes.

She leans against the door, more relaxed as she motioned with her head behind her.

"She's just over there," as casual as anything, giving nothing away.

It seems like our 'cat and mouse game' has commenced again. She knows this drives me mad, but she revels in it. I just look at her, containing my amusement.

"So, where you off to?" *Yeah*, I'm going there again, can't help myself.

"I was just catching some air, as I had some *fucker* harassing me *all* morning," she rolls her eyes before settling them firmly on *me*.

Yeah, my cock got harder. She really is the only woman I'd ever let speak to me like that. Anyone else would get a well deserved slap. But as I said, we have history and it is '*Her*' after all.

"Want me to sort them out for you?" I look at her, trying to keep a straight face, knowing full well she is talking about me.

And so the banter has well and truly begun as I see her eyes soften towards me.

Yeah, I love the fact that even though I'm truly a cunt, I can still induce *that* look in her eyes.

"I can you know? Just say the word and its sorted," I wink at her. "*So*, when are *we* going to catch up, seeing as you are going?"

Now, I see, her eyes flash, she knows she has won this round. *I gave in first you see…*

I normally do, as she is so guarded, she has walls that might never be pulled down, I see them as walls that need climbing. *So*, I take one for the team. Okay, my team, *team me*. But it works.

"*So…* Fancy a drink later?" I watch as the corners of her mouth curl into a smile.

"I might be busy," man she is cool, proper ice queen, she deserves her title, she has earned it. "Emma and I have plans."

This I know is true, as these two are joined at the hip. Have been since they met. They have this bond, a tight unbreakable one.
I can understand, seeing as I know and have seen what they are capable of. I know no matter what, Emma comes as part of '*Her*' life, anyone that enters '*Her*' life would know this too.

And one should *always* be delicate when skirting around the issue of anything Emma.

"Why don't I take the two of you out?" *Yes*, I know I am chancing my luck here.

'*She*' knows it too and is just about to punch me full force into the balls with her answer. Of course, she will be diplomatic in her special way, but it will still be a punch in the nuts neither-the-less.

"I don't think the places Em and I go to will be your sort of place," she drags her top teeth over her lower lip.

See, I told you it would be a punch in the nuts. And she is not going to recant her statement either.

"Wow," I blink, trying to hide my obvious offence. "That told me, good and fucking proper," I stare at the wheel trying to look overly offended.

"You know I didn't mean it like that," she looks sincerely at me over the mirrored lenses. "I just think you would get bored with some of the knobs at these things."

I give her one of my '*I'm unmoved by your words looks*' but this one is softer, only for her.

"I don't want you being uncomfortable that's all," she shrugs.

I watch as she pushes the trestles of blonde hair that have been annoying her, behind her ear.

"I am actually thinking of *you*," she looks to me now trying to convince me.

"So basically," I look her dead in the eye. "You don't think I am good enough for you?"

"No I don't," she laughs throwing her head in the air. "But you don't either," she shrugs as she stares me down, knowing she is hundred percent correct.

"Really?" She sees I'm highly amused by her statement.

"Yep... Afraid so," she leans into the car a little more. "You *know* **you melt** like a chocolate teapot when it comes to *me*... You know full well, you're scared of me..." Now she is really playing it up with her teasing minx mode. "I'm probably the only person **you** are actually scared of?"

Her eyes are still toying with mine, but I have to say… BINGO, she is on the ball, totally right. And I am saved by the bell again, literally as my phone rings. *Fucking phone.*

I watch as she pulls out from the window. I shake my head, *fucking phone*, I could throw the cunting thing away.

"Let me ring you later?" I lean over to see her nod her head yes. "I'll catch you later… Yes?" She nods her head again as she walks off.

I have no choice but to take the call… It's my Mrs.

I listen to my Mrs. watching '*Her,*' walking off. I'm willing for her to turn around and take one last look at me, like the other birds do… But she don't…

See, I know she wants me, but she won't make the first move and *never* will. '*She*' is too old fashioned, not like the tarts or bints that throw themselves at me.

I pull away from the kerb towards home. It's been a few nights since I've slept in my own bed.

But that doesn't stop me taking my son to school most mornings and it's me that picks him up from school everyday no matter what.

I love my boy, he is my prince, I don't want him having this life.

He is privately educated, best school in London. He will *NOT* follow in my steps if I can help it.

He is clueless as to what I do and I will keep it that way for as long as I can.

My Mrs. is quite rightly fucked off with me. I spend most of my nights, not in my own bed. She is a good woman to put up with me and my antics. But she knew what I was all about when she met me. I was a 'Big Face' in London and she loves the power.

I drive over there and spend some time at home, smoothing things over. All the while, I'm thinking of '*Her*'.

I know '*She*' has told Emma everything about *us*, she is '*her* confidant. And she is possibly presenting the idea of what I said about joining them later to her, much to Emma's disgust. I find myself staring at the phone.

I get caught, but blag my way out of it saying I have lots going on with work. By now, I don't know if she believes me or not, not that it matters. I do my own thing regardless and work always comes first.

Now, you probably don't like me much and think that *any* woman is too good for me… Even the slutty bints.
And, you're probably right?

I know I'm not good enough for '*Her*', but it's not going to stop me. God knows I've tried to stop myself, *this*, why I find myself at home with Queen Bee.

By rights and if I had got my act together, my son should have been '*Hers*'.

That would have been the perfect scenario for me. Me and '*Her*' could have ruled the world… *We still can…*

I find myself spending a few hours at home before I'm outta there. It's not long before I find myself dialing '*Her*' number. I wait with what I can only describe as baited breath. Her voice makes me instantly hard.

'*She*' would have had a great career in the sex line business. My cock gets harder thinking of her linguistic talents, knowing how many languages she speaks. And finally she answers the phone.

"Hello," she purrs, its sweet music to my ears, after hearing my Mrs. Banging-on about this and that in her nasal voice that now sounds like nails on a chalk board to me.

"So," I try to dull the excitement in my tone at hearing her. "What's the score for later?"

"Well," she pauses. And I know the ball punch is looming again by her tone. "Em and I are out tonight," I hear her breathe hard. I know she wants to see me, but she is going to play hard to get. "I just don't think," she trails off.

Yep, so I am told… I am not good enough… *This*… I already know.

"So, talk dirty to me," I laugh. "It's the least you can do seeing you've got me all hard." I hear her laughing at the other end of the phone.

"What are you like?" She laughs. "It's not even four o'clock and you want me to talk filth to you," she gasps in astonishment. There is a pause. "Hold on then, I'll grab my cigarettes."

I laugh as I hear her tell Emma she's going downstairs for a smoke.

I hear a door close as she speaks and I hear *her* footsteps descending the stairs.

The filth that is falling out of her mouth is amazing.

I can feel my tip literally fighting to get out of my suit pants. I am so *hard* right now, it's a very uncomfortable drive, and I did this all to myself, knowing full well, this would be the end result.

Before I know it, I find myself driving through the same traffic lights I saw her at this morning. I park up and see her. She is pacing outside the door, cigarette in hand and phone to her ear as she is talking into it.

My cock is so hard right now as I watch her. She tells me to stroke my tip over the fabric with my thumb. I find myself obeying her, teasing as though it was her tongue. My cock pumps a throb with excitement as I close my eyes and listen to her.

Now you see why I think of her to get hard.

My cock pumps again, at the mere thought of '*Her*'… I forget where I am, and that is, sitting in a car, in a busy crescent in London and she is *still* continuing to talk dirty to me. *I'm melting big time.*

"*So*," she purrs. "Did *that* do the trick?" She laughs as she teases me more. I can hear her taking another drag on her cigarette and then exhaling.

"*Yeah*, you always *do*," I look down at the tent that has accumulated in my trousers.

"I'm gonna have to wank that out… You've left me with a serious hard-on… Again," I laugh staring at my massive rod lining my trouser leg after some re-adjusting.

"Well that was the whole idea," I look over and see her throw her hair back like the minx she is. "Well, if you're done, I'll let you go then… My work here is finished."

"*So*, I'll call you later yes?" I pose one of those rhetorical questions. "I *would* like to see you before you go."

I look over and see she is happy at what I have said, although she keeps her tone cool, sounding blasé.

If only she knew I was actually watching her, she would skin me alive.

However, if I wasn't here, I would only have heard her response and would've had to have settled for that …

Now I *know* she likes me *more* than she lets on and *this* pleases me greatly.

It seems the years of hard graft I have put in are paying off.

This thought alone makes me laugh. Being me…

The lady killer. I can proudly boast I can get any woman into my bed or against a wall, whatever…

All except her, well until now.

My cock thumps again at the thought of it as I watch her finish her cigarette and stub it out with her foot.

"Dunno, ring me and we'll see what we are doing yes?"

See, told you she was clever, because *now* she is playing me at my *own game*.

"*Yeah*, I'll ring you," I find myself still looking at my hard cock.

"Yeah laters," and she is gone just like that. Except I get to see what she does next.

I'm disappointed to see her turn without a care in the world and go back into the building she came from.

I'm angry, I can't help it. I like to always think of her playing games and maybe being girlie after one of our chats. But then, I saw her, like she had just finished paying a bill over the phone… *Nice!!*

I feel my cock pump again, see, it's unaware of the rejection I feel.

So… I'm going to do something about it.

Angrily I pull away and find myself outside the dirty bints flat. *Yeah* the one I fucked in the arse.

As soon as she opens the door, I am backing her into her flat. Her hands are in my trousers and she is releasing my cock.

She drops to her knees and is sucking me off, before you can say 'Cockfosters'.

I look down as I watch her head slide back and forth taking my cock deep into her mouth.

My hips move in motion with her as I fuck her mouth. I feel her fingers teasing my nuts, teasing them hard. She lets my cock bounce out of her mouth with a ping as it stands to attention. She looks up at me pleased with her work.

I watch her. She has a glint in her eyes as she crawls like a cat into the sitting room, where I fucked her the day before. I follow her until she stops at the couch and motions for me to sit down.

She is immediately on my cock again, I grab her ponytail and pull her down onto my rod. Her lips are wrapped around my shaft. I slide my free hand over her back until I get to her arse cheeks.

My index finger slides under the string of her thong and I start to stroke her soft folds. She moans a series of *"Mmmmmm's"* around my cock as my fingers slip into her. I draw my hand back and forth as her head dips vigorously, as she fucks me with her mouth.

Still my fingers glide in and out of her wet snatch, I slip another in as she continues to suck me into her throat.

I slide one finger out, wet with her cream and start to tease her rim. Soon her cream is dripping, so I use it to make her rim wetter by the minute, enough for me to slip a finger with ease into it

Two in the pink and one in the stink, gets this girls engine roaring.

Once it goes, she is game for anything, and I mean anything. Maybe later, but for now I'm going to make the bint cum her arse off while she swallows my load.

I increase my speed and I slip another finger into her arse, my hand moving like an well oiled machine as she cums. I know if I keep going she's going to squirt. I increase my pace and fuck her with my hand, as she chokes on my cock, she squirts her jizz. It tips me over the edge as I pump my load deep into her throat.

My hips thrust with the last pump, I pull her down further on me, choking her with my cock, her mouth right at the base of my length.

I pull her off me by her hair, still wrapped around my fist. I breath deep, my thoughts were of 'Her' and doing this all to her. See how I like to torture myself?

So what am I doing, fucking around with other women?

Why am I not focusing all my attentions of winning '*Her*' for good?

Because **I'm not ready for her**…

Being with her means having to walk away from all of this…

The life style I have built, my reputation, everything that is *me*… I will, one day.

Every time I see her, I think that day draws closer and closer for me…

Soon I will be ready to walk, have enough money under my belt, to never have to worry about it ever again.

I'm one big deal away…

6

HERE

I'm back in my car again when I think of the other night. So close, but yet, so far…

I do believe, just one brush of her soft lips will make me succumb to her. I imagine it often, hence my little montage of her by the car. *Now* part of me is wishing I made my thoughts a reality. *You* don't know how hard it is not to just devour her. Takes all my self control… *So*, when I walk away from her, without physically putting a hand on her, I'm quite proud of myself.

So, what am I doing, fucking others, when its only her I want to fuck?

This is becoming a personal mantra for me. Plus, I like to push my limits… I have found, I possess *none*.

I've always had a taste for things…

Over the years its changed. One time it was I couldn't get enough - drugs, violence, reputation you name it… And now its sex, although I have always had a *very* healthy, probably too much of a healthy appetite for that.

My phone rings as I make my way to the club. I have a big meeting here tonight. Some major faces are coming, hence the one last big deal thing, always working towards that. It's Tommy, politely reminding me, as if he has too.

It's only a quick call and I find myself looking at my phone, wondering should I call her?

I decide against it, knowing Emma and 'Her', they'll be getting ready for tonight. No doubt she will be in some black designer number that will look like it was made for her, and Emma too. They steal the show wherever they go.

I imagine them walking into our meeting and the reaction of the other 'Faces' that will be there. Even those men would be putty in their hands.

I make it sound like they are master criminals or prostitutes or something…

If only it was as easy as that. No, these girls or women, should I say, are proper ladies.

No matter what patter any of these major 'Faces' gave, the girls would be completely immune to them, sadly, I couldn't say the same about the *'Faces'*. These girls are a different class, even though we came from the same place.

They just chose the right route by studying and working hard… Me and my lot? We chose the good old fashioned easy way… We're criminals of the highest caliber. We are as bent as nine bob notes. We'd rob the coins off your eyes.

The hours roll on and the 'Faces' start turning up. Some of the lary ones came in through the front, even spending their money down in the booths. The women flocked to them as they walked in, like they could smell the money or what's more, the power these 'Faces' have. Other 'Faces' chose to use the backdoor, which is less inconspicuous to the old bill who are cuming in their pants parked in their unmarked cars, knowing all the top 'Faces' are gathered here in *my club*.

The old Bill have been after me for years, but the stupid cunts have nothing on me and nor will they ever.

I don't take to kindly to grasses. I made sure people knew my stance on them when I first came up the lines.

I showed no mercy to the cunt, who tried grassing me up. I was looking at a two year stretch and I weren't going down, because some snitch needed his next fix.

I filled that cunt with battery acid, using his own needle.

Took ages to find a vein I could use. I was so mad, I ended up snapping the needle in the fuckers neck. That was after I smashed the fuck out of his hands and feet with a hammer. Grasses should be dealt with swiftly, I see it as *'taking out the rubbish'*. Cunt screamed like a bitch due to his fucking collapsed veins, fucking junkies.

I'm already waiting in the back room. It is dark and seedy as you can imagine, with a huge walnut conference table taking centre stage.

And I use this term 'centre stage', as this is where all the quibbles we have, are ironed out, like gentlemen. Well I say that, as no one has done a 'Martinez' since 1964.

Legend has it that Martinez stabbed one of the notorious 'Long brothers' through the eye with a pencil. 'Long', funnily enough was without 'said brother' and partner in crime that night. It was a costly lesson to the Long family, but one that put Martinez on the map and a rule of no bloodshed on meetings premises in future, a rule that has been obeyed since.

No one is frisked or patted down, *fuck no…* We're all tooled up in some shape or fashion. We know we are walking into war at any minute and we need to be prepared.

Asking anyone of us to give up our weapons would get you killed, you get my drift?
So, I am listening to two firms arguing between themselves about some petty feud they have. We all have them, some just burn a bit deeper than others.

It looks like it will kick off at any minute. I see Mickey Partridge, shit stirring as usual, cunt is like a shit magnet.

Has a true nose for hassle, guaranteed, if there is trouble, Mickey is behind it in some shape or fashion. Has been, since his hooligan days like me. But he is a 'Face' and that is why he, along with other cunts, are sitting at this table.

When the meeting finishes up, Tommy signals for Leroy to let the girls in.

I watch as they go to work on the 'Faces'. Grinding against their cocks, shaking their tits in their faces. All except Ray the Gay... *Well*, that's coz he's gay innit?

Some of the darkened corners are being used to every advantage for a quick fumble. I see Connie, one of the girls, bending over one of the high-backed chairs, while, what looks like the back of 'Slasher Robinson' doing her 'up the arse'.

To say it's colourful in here, is an understatement. But this is mild in comparison to what *can* go on with this bunch of vermin, there is no other word for them.

While the antics proceed, I find myself looking at one of them social media sites.

I see '*Her*' and Emma have checked into a nice posh club not far from here.

I have to say, I am seriously considering maybe making an impromptu appearance. Knowing them, they will have swarms of men around them like bees around honey.

That is one thing that turns me on regardless. I want the women everyone else wants, only difference with me is… **I get them**. It gets me hard watching the men falling over themselves.

But it's *me* that is either walking out with them or fucking them against a wall or in the toilets. *See*, told you this was a nasty habit of mine.

I tell Tommy to get the Range Rover ready. Its tinted windows give me some anonymity for the London Streets. Every now and then, some cunt thinks they're hard enough to have a go, to take over…

Those fuckers are dealt with swiftly too...

Normally over the roof of a very high building. It just means I have to always be aware of my surroundings at all times.

Big Dave brings the car round, he is looking to drive.

I give him one of those *'better luck next time'* looks as I snatch the keys out of his hand and make my way into the driver's seat and start the car up.

In less than five minutes I am outside the venue.

It's a private club, the membership is costly, but worth it, as I won't see any of them other cunts in here.

They wouldn't have the class to even look at this place, its well off their radar, hence why I like it here.

Here I supply 'recreational supplements', not by my own fair hand of course, no, it's been a very long time since I have directly handled things like that. I have two people here on my books, that tend to that side of things for me. Here, I'm just like any other business man who can afford the high price tag of their exclusive membership.

Now I'm wondering how they, *'Her'* and Emma are here? I'm not surprised they know of it, just wondering who has the membership…
Probably both knowing them.

I acknowledge the security chaps as I walk in, I know them well, I know everyone… And they me.

I make my way to the main bar with Big Dave, who is six foot seven, and built like the champion bare-knuckle fighter he is, complete with cauliflower ears and smashed in nose.

He shadows me, making sure he is near, just in case. Now, in a place like this, no one would have a go… No, they are all gents, or what I like to call them, thieves from the city. These fuckers are all about money, who's got what and all, old money.

It's like a proper pissing competition here, toff style with who's got the bigger yacht or estate in Scotland or wherever.

I'm nursing my scotch, leaning against the bar when I hear some jovial cheers and champagne corks popping, coming from around the oak clad columns.

I don't even need to look, to know its them.

It's confirmed when I see '*Her*' walking towards the bathrooms. Being the chancer I am, and seeing old habits are hard to die… I follow her swiftly.

Big Dave knows the score when he sees me pursuing a woman under circumstances like this.

So he follows me and makes sure, that our disturbance is minimal.

I wait momentarily until I walk into the ladies bathroom after a woman comes out. I don't particularly give a fuck if I am caught in here, that's what Big Dave is for.

When 'She' comes out of the cubical, I am sitting there in one of the fancy chairs by the huge dressing table with the ornate mirror they have for birds to fix themselves up.

She don't notice me at first as she washes her hands, it's only when she's at the dryers that she spies my reflection in the mirror in front of her.

I laugh to myself, that's the second time today I have made her jump.

'She' spins around composed and looks me dead in the eye…

"Well, well… They'll let any old riff raff in here now a days," and she laughs as she leans against the wall.

I can tell I have unnerved her, with being here, but she is taking it all in her stride as I move off the chair and walk towards her.

I can see her eyes widen with excitement, I know my cock is throbbing with it too, shame she can't see that, but maybe soon if I have my way.

I am in her personal space and she isn't batting an eyelid. *See*, love it, shows no fear even though she senses it.

I reach for her face and bring her to me. I want to taste her lips, I have imagined this too many times and regretted the opportunities I have wasted.

And my mouth is on hers. I want to kiss her slowly, savor every moment, but I find myself kissing her hungrily, as much as she is me.

We can't stop, lost in an embrace that we never saw coming. Well of course we did, but you know what I mean. The electricity between us is off the charts.

I find myself pushing up against her, pushing her back into the wall as we start into a mad frenzy. Our tongues are entwined, dancing with deviancy. I can't help but press my hard cock into her, just to let her know what she does to me.

She feels it and her eyes widen as she looks at me, smoldering with lust. I want to rip the dress off, devour her, in all her entirety.

And it's like we both then remember where we are. She pulls away from me, leaning back into the wall looking every inch the seductive vixen she is.

"Seems you have a habit of trying to score with me in the ladies loos," she laughs. "Some things never change," and her eyes narrow with pure devilment.

I laugh to myself, if only she knew half of it and my panache for fucking in the ladies bathrooms. I shrug it off casually. She's got me on that one. I move towards her again and she places her hand on my chest stopping my advances.

"We are not doing this *here*," her eyes motion '*no fucking way*'.

I find myself stepping back… *Fuck, you see? This is what she does to me.*

Any other bird and my cock would be so far up them they would only be singing '*Mmmmmm's*'.

However, this action only seems to amuse her and for the right reasons.

"I need to get back out there," her eyes motion to the door. "Em is out there." I can't help it, but move towards her again and my mouth is firmly on hers.

"I need to go," she manages to say in between the kisses we exchange.

"Fuck them," I growl as I move back on her mouth, as her tongue dances with mine. "Let them wait… As long as *I* have… *For you*."

This does the trick as she becomes ravenous, each kiss she reciprocates only makes my cock throb harder with excitement. And she can feel it too. She pulls away again, breathing hard. I can see the fire burning in her eyes and I want to be consumed by it.

I look at her, she knows I want her with every pant my breath makes. It is taking all my self control just not to take her here and now.

I find myself backing off again, putting some distance between us, as I walk towards the huge floor length mirror and fix my tie as I watch her reflection.

'*She*' is unsure, expecting me to turn around and pounce on her like the lion I am… *And I want to… So badly.*

My need to taste her again is all consuming, it's not just dangerous for her to be in here with me…

It's equally as dangerous for me.

I could well and truly get caught up in the spiders web that is *her*.

"So… What's the plan?" I ask as I turn to look at her. "Surely none of them fuckwits have your attention?" I look at her. What I am actually doing is looking for the truth in her eyes.

"No," she laughs, much to my relief. "Although I know Em is considering *us* going back to a party," I see her roll her eyes at the sheer boredom of it. She's like me, only so much bullshit, one can take.

"So… Don't go if you don't want to… Come out with me?"

I look at her quickly before turning away, I'd rather not see her reject me like she did earlier on.

"I can't," she looks at me solemnly as I try to ignore her, but it's no use. "You know the score... I go where she goes," she looks at me blankly like its written in stone, which I know it is when it comes to them. "I go, she goes," she shrugs.

"Well, maybe we can hook up when you're finished?" Now I really can't look at her, as I showed some weakness there.

See, this is what she does to me... And *now*... *Now* it's worse as I have had her tongue in my mouth and I can still taste her...

"It could be a late one," she drags her top teeth across her bottom lip. It really is taking all my self control just not to devour her again.

"You know I'm a nocturnal creature," I wink at her as I watch her face soften, my cock thumps. "You can call me anytime," I look at her. "You know this."

"But you *know* I'm not going to do that," she looks at me boldly. "I've had your number for how long?"

I don't bother answering as she is doing one of them rhetorical things on me. I just look at her blankly trying to hide my amusement at her 'cat and mouse games'.

"And how many times have I called you?"

She is looking at me with her eyebrows raised, arms folded and her fingers drumming her arrogance. *See* another thing about her that gets my cock hard, she is cocky like me, but in the right way. And she has *never* called me… Not once!

"And your point is?" I smile cheekily at her knowing I am starting another volley that could quite well end up with me walking towards her and claiming her mouth again.

She looks at me coolly, as if she is imagining the same thoughts as mine about the ending of this volley and me claiming her mouth. I see her eyes narrow, which only leads me to believe that she is…

I find myself walking towards her and taking her into my arms again.

The need to taste her is too much to bear, especially seeing as she is right in front of me.

Our hands grab at each other in our frenzy, knowing full well we can be disturbed at any time. It stokes both our fires and I have to stop myself from scooting my hand up her thigh and towards her panties.

I can't tell you how hard it is to ignore my primal urges that she has fuelled. It seems we are immersed in *'full on animal'* mode.

It is me this time that pulls back, just as she starts to stroke my cock through the fabric of my trousers.

I really don't want to have a quick fuck with her in the bogs.

Fuck no… I've waited years for *her.*

If I'm going to have *her*, I want *her* for as long as I can. I want to totally consume *her*, I want to drown in her.

"You melting again?" She moves towards me with the true prowlness of the dominate female lioness.

I do find myself melting, this bitch makes me soft in places I'm not used to, like my rock of a heart, *NOT* my cock, just pointing that out.

She is just about to tease my lips with her tongue when we hear Emma speaking or should I said questioning Big Dave.

'*She*' wanted to go out immediately, me, I wanted to see how Big Dave would handle Emma.

Big Dave is more of a man's man if you get my drift and his language of that, is fists.

Like kids we listen at the door, I watch as she presses her ear against the wood and giggles as she hears Big Dave get all tongue tied as he tries to explain that the toilets are having a minor maintenance at the moment.

Pretty impressive eh?

Especially, as he really is not the sharpest knife in the drawer, if you get my drift.

I watch, finding myself looking at her mouth, it's inviting and I want another taste...

So… I reach out and grab her face gently, pulling her into me.

She kisses me back, her eyes *are closed!!*

7

HIGH FOR THIS

Suddenly she pulls away from me, I feel the heat of her lips leave mine.

"I can't do this," she looks up at me. "You are not going to *fuck me* in the ladies toilets," she stares at me with certainty. "What am I talking about?" She brings her hands to her temples bemused. "Can you hear what I'm actually saying... *Me*... Sleep with *you*?" *Yeah that one hurt like a right kick in the nuts with steel-toe capped boots.*

"Don't plan on getting much sleep with you," I wink, cocky as *fuck*. She knows I mean it too.

"You're incorrigible," she smirks at me shaking her head. "And Emma is going to *lose* the plot with your chap, if I don't get out there and save him."

I place my hands either side of her shoulders against the wood of the door, entrapping her. I am face to face with her, she stands there, as brazen as anything. My cock throbs in her presence, I feel the heat off her breath and I want her... *Bad.*

The scent of '*Her*' fills my nostrils and my testosterone kicks in, surging through me. Her eyes glint as she breaths in the chemistry between us. I feel the animal in me come forth, while my prey waits for me to strike my death blow.

"Stay with *me* tonight," I growl leaning into her. I feel her skin tingle beneath me as I do.

Being honest, I can't believe I'm being this forward with her. But I can't help myself. I want to feel her bare skin against mine.

I want to hole up in some five star hotel and live off room service with her for the rest of my life.

And by the look in her eyes, the feeling seems mutual.

Before I know it, my lips are on hers again as we devour each other hungrily, knowing at anytime, Emma will come bounding in through the door, with a distasteful look due to our embrace.

Me, I think it's as *hot as fuck*. I like the idea of getting caught, it only heightens *my* pleasure. As you can probably tell, I don't really have any hang ups about sex, except for me getting fucked in the arse that is.

I've fucked many a girl, in a room *full* of people. It don't bother me. I can't tell you how many meals I've had at some very fine establishments, whilst some bint is sucking me off under the table. I have tag teamed with some of the lads, *fuck it*, when you have a bint who wants more cock then she can handle. Yeah, too fucking right, I'm up for some of that.

But *this* fucking woman, the *one* who is making my cock want to burst through my trousers and cum in her, really rings my bell.

She pulls away breathless from my mouth. We can hear Big Dave has lost his battle with Emma.

She is hurling insults at him and making curt remarks about his thuggish ways.

"I can't," she quickly smoothes her dress down in preparation for Emma's appearance, breaking her eye contact with me.'

I disengage from her, putting a little bit of distance between us and sit back into the chair, I first sat in.

"I don't know what Em's plans are," she gives me one of her apologetic looks.

"Call me after then?" I shrug. "It's not like I'm going to be busy," she looks at me, giving me one of those 'Oh yeah, *right*' looks.

I don't blame her, seeing as it has been my business in some shape of form, that has been a good reason for *us* not getting together.

"Well that's me cancelling my membership then," Emma looks directly at me. "They will let any old *riff raff* in here nowadays."

"Funny, '*She*' said the same thing," I motion with my head at '*Her*' and then back up at Emma, with a '*pleased with myself*' look.

"*Hmmmmm*," she taps her foot as she looks between the two of us.

Emma knows something has gone on. She knows the whole story of *us*. But we are both styling it out and I must say, we are doing a blinding job keeping our composure, considering the wildfire that was happening only moments before she interrupted us.

I can only imagine the squeals of Emma later, when '*She*' tells her, about our swaray in the bathroom and how Em interrupted us and how clueless she was as to what *had* happened when she walked in.

"You ready?" Emma looks at '*Her*' who is nodding her head yes. "Sorry to break up the party," Emma looks at me with a devious smile. "But *we* have a party of our *own* to go to."

"Yeah I know, '*She*' was just saying," I flippantly reply like I don't give a shit. I seriously should get an Oscar for being Best Actor. "Have a nice time," I look at them as they both leave the bathroom.

And I am left there, alone, sitting in this poxy chair. I only sit there for a moment, before I join Big Dave to go back to the bar. As we pass an alcove, I spy them with a group of men. I'm not in the least surprised. I try not to look, but can't resist and catch '*Her*' looking at me as I pass them by.

I am trying to play it cool, my walk would make a fantastic '*slow walk*' clip. All I want to do is grab her by the hand and get the fuck out of here and take her to the first five star hotel we find.

I head straight for the bar and order a large scotch and knock it back. As I slam the glass down I order another. I know Big Dave is looking at me. No matter how 'punch drunk' he is from the bare-knuckle fighting, he knows enough to know I am rightly fucked off and he knows, it's because of 'the sort' and her mate, the one who gave him an earful.

I ignore him as he asks if "*You're alright Gov?*" And knock back the scotch and order again.

To say **I am pissed-off**, is an *understatement*. **I** am *not* used to getting knocked back. I turn around, to lean on the bar, just in time to see '*Her*' and her party pass me as they go to leave. She looks at me again and is ushered out by the 'chap' who is trying to get all pussy-fingers with her.
God, I want to go over and lump him in the face. Like *he* has a fucking chance with '*Her*'.

I watch like 'Sophie's choice' as the door closes.

I gulp back my drink angrily and head for the door with Big Dave following me. I hand him the keys as we walk to the Range Rover.

I'm too angry to drive, I'll probably mow some fucker down who would be stupid enough to step out in front of me.

We make our way back to my club, that sort Kelly with the big tits will be sent to my office. I'm livid and a hard, dirty fuck and a few lines of coke, will do the trick, sort me out.

I've just had a line or two, when I hear a knock at the door. I tell her to get 'her arse' in here and she does, wearing one of those tartan skirts that is barely covering her arse cheeks. Her tits are heaving out of the tiny t-shirt she is barely wearing, perfect for me to bury my face and cock in.

She walks in and sits in front of me on my desk, legs spread.

I sit there, wondering why the fuck she isn't down, noshing on my cock, but I can soon render that.

"Suck my cock," I command as I look up at her. She slides off my desk and onto her knees.

She makes it look like an art form as she unzips my trousers and releases my cock.

Her mouth is sliding up and down my shaft, my hand, resting on the back of her head as I watch it bob up and down.

I'm rock hard, my cock is throbbing as her tongue glides and teases over it. I see her slip her hand between her thighs and into her panties as she rubs her clit. That just makes my cock thump so I pull her up and quickly turn her around and bend her over my desk, pulling her panties to the side and slip my cock into her wet pussy.

I am smashing the fuck out of her, when I have the taste for another line. I pull out of her, telling her to "*stay there and don't move*".

I lean down into the desk drawer and pull out a pack and the credit card I use for chopping. She looks back and asks for a taste herself. I set two lines up for her and tell her to wait, while I form two big fuckoff lines for me, on her arse cheek, telling her "Not to move." I snort both lines and feel the charge.

"Go on then," I nod to her.

As Kelly snorts hers, I slide my cock hard back into her, feeling her pussy squeeze tightly on my shaft and I fuck her like a jackhammer. She is loving it, with her '*Ooohhh's* and *Ahh's'* as I smash against her.

I'm grinding hard into her when my mobile rings. I glance down and see '*Her*' name flashing on the screen.

My cock is still in Kelly when I answer.

"What's up?" I know something ain't right, she never calls me. I listen intently. "I'm on my way."

I hang up , pull out of Kelly and fix myself. She looks up at me taken aback, as to why I am finishing our fuck, before time.

"Laters babe," I zip myself up and head for the door as she looks at me, fixing herself, and I am gone…

I motion to Big Dave and he doesn't hesitate in following me out. We walk to the Range Rover, he still has the keys from earlier and I have no qualms about letting him drive. We get in and head off to the address '*She*' gave me. I tell him to put his foot down.

He knows there's a reason, I'm sure he is assuming we are going into a battle of some sort and he is absolutely right.

I'm anxious, we get there in ten minutes.

Big Dave has just pulled up to the kerb, when I am out of the car and bounding up the steps to the swanky stucco fronted terrace house with its porticoed entrance. I press all the buzzers to the apartments which are set over four floors with the palm of my hand. I hear someone random pick up their intercom.

"Pizza Delivery," I say, as I hear a long buzz and the front door lock releases.

I burst through it, hearing Big Dave, telling me *"to wait for him."* But I am gone, up the stairs like lightening. I get to one of the doors and type a quick message, press send, then I wait …

Big Dave looks at me, He is clueless as to what the fuck is going on. I'm hardly a big talker in situations like this, but he knows it's *on*, whatever it is behind door number three…

I wait and hear raised, heated voices coming from behind the door over the loud 'shit music' that is playing.

"Let us out," I hear Emma, sounding very authoritive.

I hear them taunting her with their wanky, posh accents, sounding like they fell *off* the bus at Eton or whatever.

I want them fucking horrible cunts who have sticks shoved up their arses, to feel my fists something bad. *They have messed with the wrong person, when they messed with 'Her'.*

I hear the girls again trying to reason with the pricks to let them go. All the while I look at Big Dave, who is ready to go through that door like it's made of wet tissue paper. He is just waiting for the go ahead from me. I hear raised voices again and what I can only deem to be horse-play.

That is our cue and I give the nod to Big Dave to tear the door down, which he does with one shoulder.

Big Dave and I burst through in time to see these chino wearing wankers, surrounding the girls like a pack of wolves. I don't think twice as I chin the first cunt I see and as he hits the ground I move on to deck the next. The girls have made their way out the door and I'm shouting for them to wait downstairs. They don't need to see what is going on up here. Big Dave and I cut through them like a 'hot knife through butter', until there is one still untouched…

He is the cunt who was trying to play pussy fingers with '*Her*' at the club… I'm going to enjoy this.

I walk towards him menacingly, I have been saving him for last. He knows that I am after *his* blood, fucker pisses himself.

What is it with people pissing themselves?

He is leaning against the glass of the window, his legs are shaking, it's quite visible, along with the piss stain trickling down the front of his chino trousers. That's when I see the girls down on the street shivering. I look at the sniveling posh cunt, as I hold him by the throat.

"You fucked with the *wrong girls* this time wanker," I snarl into his face. Fucker starts to piss himself again.

I look down at the puddle that is beneath our feet. I look to Big Dave.

"Is he having a fucking laugh?" I watch as Big Dave, shrugs his shoulders shaking his head. "You dirty cunt," I snarl again. "These are new shoes."

I release my grip seeing as he is turning red and his eyes are starting to bulge like a cocker spaniels.

"You know what *cunt*… I've got better things to do than to stand in your piss," I look at him as he stumbles back, trying to catch his breath. He starts clutching his throat as I stare him down. "Fuck you *cunt*, you ain't worth it." I turn and start walking, stepping over his fuckwit mates. "D… Sort *him*," I command as I walk the fuck out the door.

As I walk down the stairs I hear him begging, pleading to Big Dave. I laugh to myself, as if Big Dave will go easy on him. He is deaf with them big ole cauliflower ears of his.

I make my way out onto the street to the girls.

"What the fuck happened there?" I look between the two, before settling my eyes onto '*Her*'.

"Don't," '*She*' looks at me as Emma pipes up.

"They just got a bit rowdy, that's all," Emma tries to defend her decision to go back with the guys.

I can only give her one of those *'Are you fucking kidding me'* looks as Emma stands there brazenly. Does she realize that I have practically broken down a door to save them? *Okay, well, Big Dave did, but you get my point?*

"Then why am I here?" I look at her blankly. "Look, you want a lift or what?" I look to *'Her'*, *'She'* nods her head and gives Emma a look.

"Em," she looks at her.

See I know how 'independent' they both are. This is why I don't understand *them*, getting into a spot of bother like this.

I can see Emma is going to argue, for what? I don't know, maybe she was outnumbered and thinks her odds are better winning an argument with me. Clever bitch, she knows I'll be on my best behaviour for *'Her'* so Emma is taking liberties.

All of a sudden, we hear a girly scream coming from above us.

Big Dave has that chino, wearing wanker, hanging out his own window by his ankles.

We can clearly hear him begging for his life and for Big Dave not to let go.

We even hear about the safe he has in his bedroom, and how very happy he would be to part with the cash he has in it, if only he could come back in from the window.

The girls look to me with horror on their faces. I try to stifle my laugh.

Me? I think this is fucking hilarious. It's really quite a comical scene. *However*, I am being good, and on my best behaviour, as I said. I can see the girls are clearly distressed by this.

"I'll sort it," I look at her reassuringly as she nods. "The car is over there," and I motion with my head to the Range Rover parked two cars away from us. "The doors are open, make yourselves comfortable," they nod as I start to make my way back into the building.

I know Big Dave won't drop him without my say-so. But the mention of a safe *and* money? *Yep… Of course* I'm going to take advantage and have a taste of that… So back in I go…

In less than ten minutes, Big Dave and I are walking back to the car.

I have a nice thick envelope in my inside breast pocket, full of cash. Around twenty thousand, which is not a bad turn out for the night.

I don't even need to look back to know that chino wearing wanker is watching from his third floor window, accompanied by a few of his wanky mates.

When I went back up, none of them wankers had the minerals to step up and say anything.

Of course they wouldn't with Big Dave still up there. It was something I pointed out to that fucker, as Big Dave pulled him back in from the window. One fucker even offered what was in his wallet, I looked at him and asked him;

"What? Do you really think you're getting turned over?" Poor cunt nearly shit himself.

I just made it clear that we weren't here for that, we had come to rescue the girls as the wankers looked like a rape party waiting to happen. He then made the mistake of saying the girls were only *'high paid tarts'*. That got him a smash in the bollocks with my fist.

I think I made my point clear and that if they called the plods, *we*, as in *me* and *Big Dave* would *be back*, along with a few of my mates.

And, after taking each of their business cards, I now know, where *each* and every *one* of them worked. *Yeah*, I think they got the message *loud and clear*.

Before getting into the front with Big Dave, I checked on the girls, seeing if they were okay after their ordeal. We drove them back to Emma's, well around the corner as Emma didn't want me knowing where she lived. I chuckled to myself, if only she knew…

Bar that, there is very little talk on the drive back.

We pull up and I do the gentlemanly thing and open the car door for the girls. Being the clever fucker I am, I went to Emma's side and let her out first knowing full well, '*She*' would be the last out, and that would give me a chance to speak to her.

Fair play to Emma, she gave us the time to talk, standing back.

"So, *no* hotel tonight then?" I look at '*Her*' as she nods. "*Fucking typical,*" I shake my head, I shove my hands into my trouser pockets. This is to stop me. I want to touch her face and reassure her that I mean what I say. "Are you and I ever going to be able to cut a break?"

"Not tonight, but maybe next time?" *'She'* looks down at the ground. Like me, she can't look too long and I can only presume that she is wanting a repeat of 'our moment' in the bathroom.

"When do you get back?" *God, I hate myself, I sound like one of those needy fuckers.* "I mean, what time do you leave for the airport tomorrow?" *Yeah now I sound like a right needy mug, and I expect I'll get worse.*

"11am," *'She'* looks up at me, it's like she knows what I'm going to say next.

"I'll drive you to the airport if you want?" *See*, can't stop myself. Now I'm only hoping she will say yes.

"Yeah, that will be good, it will save me from getting a taxi," she smiles up at me making me melt on the spot like a teenage boy asking for his first date. "But if you can't make it, phone me will you? Don't have me waiting for you like a plank if you're a no show."

"You know I wouldn't do that to you?" *'She'* gives me a look. "Ah come on, that wasn't my fault, you know how it is?" *'She'* nods her head, she knows the score, it wasn't my fault, she knows this.

"I know… I know, don't try and make me feel guilty, *I'm* the injured party on *that* not you… *You're* the *tosser* that could have had, at least *some* courtesy and called me, rather than letting me wait like a plum."

'*She's*' 100% correct of course. I *should* have and I can't argue the point. I hear Emma, clearing her throat politely, telling us, our time is up.

"Suppose I better let you two go then?" '*She*' nods. "*So*… I'll be here tomorrow for 11 then?" I know I will have her on her own for the drive, we can do all the chit chat then on the way there.

Emma coughs, breaking the eye contact we have. *God*, I just want to grab her and kiss her. I want the hotel, the works.

But I hear Emma coughing not so quietly this time, so I step back, before making my way back to the front passenger seat. I know they won't move an inch, until we go, so I instruct Big Dave to pull off. It's not like I don't know now, where '*She's*' based when she is over here.

I have offered to set her up here, but she won't have none of it. I have tried after everyone of her failed relationships.

She only laughs at me, telling me she can look after herself. I know she isn't short of a bob or two, she is always working and earns fantastic money. She'd have to, to have the lifestyle she does.

I'm silent on the drive back to the club, it's not like Big Dave is the biggest talker, which suits me fine. But I am *fucking angry*, even though I have twenty 'big ones' in my pocket for doing nothing.

Yeah of course I'm going to bung Big Dave some, if it weren't for him, I wouldn't have this wad of notes in my pocket.

By the time we get back, the club is still in full swing.

I make my way back up to my office, telling Tommy to send Kelly with the tits, back up. I have a nice pile of coke to get through. I need to get my fuck on, seeing as my plans for tonight have been fucked up because of them chino wearing wankers…

But… I am 20k up, I suppose…

8

REAL LIFE

I've just dropped my son off to school. My phone is in my hand and *yeah,* you guessed it, I'm calling '*Her'*.

"*Well good morning,*" 'She sounds chirpy, and I'm surprised she has answered my call. "I suppose your calling to cancel… I knew you would melt," she laughs.

"*Actually,*" I chuckle. "I'm calling to see if you want breakfast?" '*She's'* silent, I guess she is shocked. I probably would have thought the same thing. "That's before I drop you off at the airport of course," *yeah* I am sounding rather smug.

I can hear the cogs in her head turning, she's wondering if I'm taking the piss.

"Look, if you're too busy packing... I just thought, what with how last night went, maybe we could catch up... *Plus...* I'm fucking starving," I laugh.

"Well... *I never...* And there was me thinking you were going to melt like an ice cream cone in the desert sun."

See... Such a cheeky bitch, but she does make me laugh, as well as making my cock *really* hard.

"*So...* I just dropped my boy off to school... I can pick you up where we dropped you off last night if you like?"

Did you like that? Clever, aren't I?

"Errmm, I dunno, I still have to pack... Oh go on then, as long as I'm at the airport for 1pm, we should be okay... How long will it take for you to get here?"

"Probably about 10 minutes, depending on traffic, it can be a bitch near you with that poxy roundabout... Maybe 20 minutes tops."

"Yeah, okay... I should be finished by then. Why don't you ring me when you're here and we can take it from there?"

"No Emma this morning?" I ask. "She can come too." *See*, I'm fishing for information.

"*No*," she laughs. "She had to go to work," she giggles. "*Just you and me*... Do you think you can handle that?"

"Now *you're* just taking the piss," I laugh. "The real question you should be asking is... Can you handle *me*?" *God I love bantering with her.*

"*Yeah... Yeah...* You're *funny*, you really should look at possibly doing a comedy night at your club, you could be the star performer," she laughs mockingly.

"*Fuck off will ya?*" I can't even think of something snappy to say back at her. She's always on the ball. She's clearly won this one, and I didn't even let her. "*Anyway*... I'm en route...What you wearing?"

"*Why* are you asking me *that*?" Now I have her attention. I can imagine she's giving that look of bewilderment, when she goes into Elvis mode with her top lip.

"Well, a dress or skirt would make it very handy in taking advantage of you… Trousers on ladies aren't that easy to work around if you get my drift? *Just saying*," I am chuckling, but at the same time *I'm* perfectly serious.

"Now **you're** taking the piss," she laughs. "Let me go. so I can finish up packing."

"I thought you women were supposed to be good at multi-tasking?"

"*Seriously*?" She laughs, no doubt she is shaking her head at my antics. "Ring me when you're here." And she hangs up.

Well, that told me. I am still amused by the time I park up. I'm lucky enough to find the same parking space from last night. I'm going to take this as a sign… *A good one*.

I find myself picking up my phone and dialing her number, like an eager beaver.

"Well, you all packed?" I spurt out before she even says hello.

"Well *hello* to you too," she laughs sarcastically. "I will be, give me a few minutes."

"How much *did* you bring?" I say sarcastically.

"I'm packed, I'm just doing a walk through, making sure I don't leave anything here, you *cheeky fucker*," she sighs. "*Plus*, it's good to keep *you* waiting," she laughs deviously. "It will do you good."

"Fuck that... I've waited *long enough*," I laugh.

I find myself wondering what floor she's on and looking at the windows to see if I can see her pass one. And I do, she's on the second floor, I watch her, presumably go from room to room and reappear, as she still talks to me.

"Oh *have you* now?" She laughs minx like. "Maybe *not* long enough," I hear another door close and see her disappear back in the direction I had first seen her. "*Anyway*, looks like I am ready to go… I'll see you in a minute or two."

"Do you want any help with your bags?" I feel my face wince, as the words fall out of my mouth. *You see, this is the shit I'm talking about… It's like, I can't stop myself.*

"No, you're alright, I can manage… *You* can put them into the car though," a peace keeping offer from her.

"Get your skates on then... I'm *fucking famished*," I have to keep up my bad boy rep after all.

"Okay, see you in a mo then... You melt," she laughs and she's gone...

I wait and watch as she appears at the front door and then walks down the steps. I actually had to stop myself from getting out of the car and going to help her. *See*, that's the making me wanting to be the better man thing, she does.

I know I am playing with fire everytime I communicate with her. *Boy… Do I like fire.*

I like things that I'm not supposed to, always have, hence why I am, who I am.

As she approaches the Jag, I get out and take her bags, putting them in the boot. There is a moment when I think *'fuck it'* and actually contemplate whether I should kiss her, devour her there and then, hence why the bags are now in the boot.

I walk round and open the door for her. In fairness to me, I do have manners and know how to treat a lady… I just wouldn't class any of the bints I've fucked as ladies, *far from it*.

She's impressed, like I knew she'd be, as she slips into the front passenger seat. She sees me looking at her legs. It's not like I can help it, she's always had great legs, and the fact she's wearing a business suit, with a skirt just above the knee. *Of course* when she sits down, it rises to her thighs nicely. I know my eyes are going to be more on her legs, than the road.

As I close the door she watches me, she raises her eyebrows and I watch her eyes narrow, as she smiles up at me, in minx mode. I walk around to the driver's side and get in.

I can't help but focus on those legs, I'm sure she's even shimmied it up a little more while I was getting in. I find myself turning to her to talk.

"So, where do you want to go for breakfast?" I look at her I'm fighting the urge to lean across and kiss her. "We can go up town... Savoy or wherever you want?"

"*Hmmm*," she looks at me, a naughty smile on her face. "I don't really *do* breakfast... But, I will have a cup of coffee or three."

"You're not helping," I laugh as she looks at me.

"*Now* you should know better... I'm not *here* to make your life easy," she drags her bottom lip across her teeth in a seductive way.

My poor cock has no chance as it starts to spring to attention.

She just oozes sex appeal, it's natural for her. I find myself licking my own lips as I remember the taste of '*Her*' and imagine my tongue fighting with hers.

"What times your flight?"

"3pm," she laughs. "Why?"

"Do you have to go back today?" I look at her as I gauge her reaction.

She wasn't expecting that.

"I mean... What are you actually going back for? *And* come to think of it... Why haven't you moved back to London yet? You have no ties?"

She's tongue tied, surprised I've hit her with this and I haven't even started the engine. Being honest, I am a bit too. But I am curious.

"*Errr... Wow*," she shakes her head. "I wasn't expecting that... I'd at least thought you would have waited until I had stirred my coffee," she shrugs sarcastically.

"Well, your answer, will help me determine where we go?" *Yeah one of them rhetorical things, ball is back in her court.*

"Why do you have to make things so difficult?" She glances at me shaking her head.

Now I know I am giving her one of those '*You fucking what*' looks.

"Look, stay a few more days?" She looks at me. "Stay at a hotel of your choice... My shout and **I'll** pay for your return ticket, *first class of course?*"

"*But of course,*" she laughs mockingly.

"I'm serious," I look at her. "*Even for a few more days...* Or longer? Like for good."

"What and wait for *you* to *call*?" She smiles seductively at me.

"*Yeah*, something like that," the look *'She'* is giving, is melting me big time. I start to feel myself *fall* into that web of hers.

"*What, stay anywhere?*" She coos teasingly.

"Yep... *Anywhere* you want..."

"And... How often would I see you?" She leans forward a little relaxing more into the seat, teasing me.

"Well... I'd try and stay with you as much as I can, at first" I flash her a devilish smile.

"As much as you can?" I nod, as she breaks into a smile, which makes my cock pump with excitement.

I'm feeling encouraged, this could be happening. I actually feel myself getting a little excited.

"*No thank you*," she smiles, as she sits back into the seat and puts on the seatbelt. "Anyway... I have meetings scheduled for tomorrow... *So no-can-do* I'm afraid," she turns to me, enjoying the look of *'momentary shock'* on my face. "I had you going there for a minute didn't I?" She laughs.

If it wasn't her, I would seriously have given someone a slap for that. *Bitch* had me going there. I was so hooked on that line of hers... I was nearly in the net.

"Funny, *fucking funny*," I shake my head. "But **I am** serious."

"I know *you* are," she smiles back still teasing the fuck out of me. "But I *do* have work. I have meetings tomorrow," she looks sincerely at me. "Honest I do, if I'd have known your plans, I could have rescheduled."

"So *do it*," I shrug looking at her. "You work for yourself?"

"Not as simple as that... *You* of all people should know that," she touché me.

I can only shake my head, of course she's right.

I've had to rearrange and cancel so many things, not only with her, but throughout my life. Even the night my son was born. I only got there by the skin of my teeth... *But*, I *was* there to see him come into this world.

You see, it times like this, when I hate the choices I made. But I made them, and I can't turn the clocks back. Every time I try to scale down, it pulls me back in, and possibly further and further each time, hence why I know, I have to get out of the game sometime soon...

"So, coffee?" I know I can work on her, over breakfast.

I watch her nod in agreement, as I press the button and the engine purrs into motion. I pull into the London traffic. It was at a set of traffic lights when the idea came to me. I knew exactly where I was going to take her.

'*She*' says nothing until we start heading out of London, heading for Heathrow airport.

"Trying to get rid of me so quickly?" '*She*' looks at me bewildered. "*Wow,* nice way to make someone feel special," she laughs sarcastically.

I laugh at her shaking my head, humoured by her, as I watch the road.

"I thought being closer to the airport would leave *us* with more time together, *and* no stress for *you*," she's surprised. "You still don't like flying?"

I glance at her and see a smile form on her face. That will mean extra brownie points and I know she keeps tabs. At the moment, I'm currently running at a deficit, so I badly need these points.

"You remembered?" She looks at me, still pleasantly surprised.

"Of course I did," I chuckle. "You tell me everytime you have to fly," I look over at her. "And you fly... *A lot!*" She laughs flabbergasted.

"Didn't realise that I did, I must speak to you *way too* much then?" Her eyes flash deviancy.

"Do we now?" I look at her again. "*Personally*, **I'd** like to speak to you *more... Actually...* I'd really like to do a lot more than speak."

"I'm sure you would," her eyes narrow seductively.

God, my cock is starting to throb... What I would give just to check into a room right now with her.

"I would... And I would ruin you," it's my turn now to flash a deviant smile. "I would *own* every part of you," I find myself, licking my bottom lip just thinking it.

"Oh would you now... I think you're forgetting something?" She purrs.

"And what's that?" I look at her, my eyebrows raised questioning.

"You know it would be me that would be *'owning you'...* You know I make you crumble... I'm," she flashes her vixen eyes at me. "*I'm* you're kryptonite."

"Kryptonite?" She nods. "That would make me Superman then?" I shrug blasély. "I can live with that."

Before we know it, we are at one of the airports hotels. I park up and we get out and walk towards the hotel with her luggage in tow.

Now, what I would really like to do, is to go up to the reception desk and check in.

However, we walk to the dining room and take a seat at a quiet table in the corner. It's discrete, but we can see the comings and goings, I'm impressed at her choice of table location. We don't even have time to read the menu, when a pretty waitress comes to take our orders.

"You're an eager beaver love," I laugh. "We've only just sat down, you'll have to give us a few minutes," I smile politely up at her.

See, me being on my best behaviour. I have to make the best of every opportunity I have with her, as I said, brownie points. I look to '*Her*' and she is impressed with my gentlemanly behaviour... Okay, it is for me with my normal banter.

We watch as the waitress totters off then ponder over the menu. *Of course, what I want ain't on the menu.*

"So... What do you fancy?" I look over the menu with a impish look. "See anything thing you like?" I see her laughing to herself, trying to hide behind the menu card. "*I* know *I do*," I place the menu card back onto the table and boldly look at her.

"*Hmmmmm*," she pretends to look, just as the waitress comes back round.

"Are you ready to order?" She beams as she smiles between the pair of us.

"Yeah, I'll have the full English and a pot of tea," I smile, then look over to '*Her*', as does the waitress.

"Cappuccino please," she smiles up to the girl, who nods her head and heads back to where she came from.

"So, what the hell happened last night?" I look at her. "I don't understand how two clever girls like yourselves got into a situation like that?"

"It wasn't like that," she sighs shaking her head. "They just got a bit rowdy, you know, the coke bowls were overflowing," I nod. "They didn't like the fact I didn't partake." I nod again.

"It sounds stupid, but because of me not wanting the coke... One thing lead to another and they wanted to carry out a body search," I look at her, my eyes wide. "One paranoid plank, thought *I was undercover* and wearing a wire," she shook her head laughing at the ridiculousness of it all. "As I said to them...'What.. You want to frisk me'? Or how did he say it?" And then she mimics the posh cunts voice. "I say, let's give her a cavity search," she rolls her eyes.

I can feel the anger in me rise. *If only I had known this last night.*

Mind you... It's a good job I didn't... Or, I would have let Big Dave drop that fucker on his head, from that third floor window, twenty grand or not.

"We could handle it to a certain point, but then *'they'* became a very *hands on mob*," she looks at me and sees my fists clenching as my arms rest on the carver chair. "As I said, all was okay... We took it as high jinks, but one chap was quite aggressive and unfortunately seemed to be the ringleader of the pack. *Em* and I locked ourselves in the bathroom... And I called you, *Em*, didn't want me to, she said we would be able to handle them...

... *I* didn't see the point in putting ourselves in an *unnecessary situation* like that, hence, my call to you," she looks at me sheepishly.

"I was surprised... You *never* call me," I smile warmly at her. "But I'm glad you did."

I know I am, as I feel my face changing. That 'hard look' I have perfected over the years, is, *my face!!* And now, I must look like a 'right soppy cunt'. *See*, this is what she does to me...

She smiles at me, but I know it is one of regret. She's too proud to let me know what is going on. I am forever telling her that I want the *real her*, like how she is *with me* and don't need to have them walls up. But they've been up so long, she don't even know when she is doing it.

Whenever I do get to know her more, I find myself insatiable for *'Her'*, I want more and more. *She's like an onion, I think I will forever peel back the layers... Only to find more.*

Again, this is something I find utterly interesting. It was only up until a couple of years ago when I told her some of my secrets and she me, that things changed between us.

I laugh thinking about it, as we both were completely unaware of what was going on.

I know that is *when* she started to see me in a new light. Before she was a mate that used to fuck around with me, and I say that as you have to remember we have never consummated *US*. The closest we got, was last night. Fitting really, as this *all* started in the toilets.

Our order arrives and the friendly waitress serves us and leaves. We find ourselves reminiscing, about when we very first met. We find ourselves reminiscing about when we first met at the childminders and she's reminding me how me and another lad, hid her beloved teddy bear

As she recalls the story, I find myself remembering hiding it behind the couch, also her trying to get him back all day.

I feel a proper cunt now, knowing what I know now and how that teddy was her only comfort. 'Her' and her dad, moved from family members to friends houses, *a lot*. That was the one console she had, in her shitty life, and me being the little cunt that I was, even then... I must have smelled her vulnerability and preyed on her. I do remember her being a meek and mild child.

Not like the tough little fucker I was. I was fingering birds at the age of nine and lost my virginity at nine and a half.

I even tormented her in junior school, up until she got tits, then I tormented her in a different way.

I watch as she sips on her cappuccino, and she watches me eat. As you know, I normally like to eat in peace and am a man of very little words, at a time like this. *However*, not with her. Here, I am chatting like the sun will 'forever shine' on me, like it is today.

I watch as the sunlight cascades in through the windows casting a morning glow around her, almost like she is illuminated. It makes me want to do this with her forever...

"So, what do you want out of life?" I look at her as I place my knife and fork down on my empty plate. "You've been married."

"Got the divorce," she laughs as she continues to sip on her cappuccino.

"So what do you want... Where do you want to be in five years time, for instance?" I watch her face as she ponders her answer.

"Room service," she laughs as I look at her mystified. "I want to wander the world, and do it, living off room service," she smiles with conviction.

"I could do that," I stare at her, nodding my agreement with her plan. "You know how I feel about you don't you?" She looks at me sternly.

"Don't, don't say that," she looks at me dead in the eye. "You can't say shit like that to me... I'm not one of your stupid bints... Who will fall for your shit pillow talk or whatever you want to call it."

"I'm just putting it out there... And I'm telling you honestly, about how I..."

I don't get a chance to finish as I watch her looking over at the reception, obviously distracted and no longer listening to me.

"What's up?" I turn to look.

"Looks like we have company from the boys in blue," and she motions with her head at the two obvious looking detectives who stand out like sore thumbs, in their stereotypical cheap suits as they show their badges.

"You need to go," I look to her and find *'She'* is already standing and holding the pull handle of her case.

She smiles at me as I nod and starts walking. I watch as the detectives stand back and let '*Her'* out the door. They watch her arse, as the gorgeous looking business woman sashays out through the lobby and out the doors, before they make their way towards me. I am drinking my tea as they arrive at my table.

"Well, well, Detective Inspector Jacobs... I see you're with your wanking hand today," I smirk acknowledging his colleague. "What brings you here this fine morning... Off on your holidays are we?"

I watch as him and his colleague eyeball me. They *fucking hate me*, especially Jacobs. He has had it in for me, for years. He has never been able to pin anything on me. I am his *nemesis*, his golden egg. He wants me so bad he can taste it. We too have history, a long history.

I see him look at the table and observe the contents...

"*Company?*" he looks at me after seeing the lipstick on the cappuccino cup. He's seen that I've watched him clock it too.

"Nah Jacobs... It's my shade, didn't you know? Looks even better around the base of my cock," I look at him. "Why don't you go and put some on, like a good girl... Then, you can nosh me off ... You pig cunt."

I suppose that was a *step too much*, as the next thing is, Jacobs and his wanking hand of a colleague have cuffed me and are bringing me in for questioning.

As they cart me to their vehicle I spot '*Her*', getting on the hotel shuttle bus to the airport. As they bung me in the back seat, I watch the bus pull off, I taunt the wankers;

"Lads, if you wanted a rough and tumble all you had to do was ask," I look at them menacingly. "You know I'm gonna call my brief and I will be out before tea-time. It will be another waste of time for you Jacobs and *I'm sure* your governor is getting well fucked off with *all* your cock-up's? By the time my brief has finished with you two, the front desk will seem like a fucking dream job... You'll be emptying out slop buckets until you retire, you cunts."

I sit back and laugh. *Fucking work has come between us again.* And now with the old Bill turning up, that is going to unnerve her.

I can't think about that now though. Now I have to listen to these two fuckwad, dickheads in the front, thinking all their birthdays have come at once. I can't remember what they are charging me with. Don't matter either way, nothing I've done, will stick or be traced back to me. I am more than careful with everything I do.

But either way my brief 'Simon Hammond' will be getting a call from me. And his law firm will have to do some *actual* work for a change. They represent me, my business concerns and associates.

They have done, for quite a while.

That's why the old Bill hate me and trust me when I tell you, they hate Simon Hammond and his legal crew, just as much.

So it looks like I'm in for a fun afternoon, shame it wasn't spent with her. Instead, I am in a pokey cell, waiting for them fuckers to start their questioning...

9

IT WAS LONDON

I'm brought up from my cell to the interview room, where Simon Hammond is sitting at the table waiting for me.

He is a lanky piece of piss, with strawberry blond hair, looks like the weasel he is, but never the less, a fucking magnificent brief. Some of the scrapes he's got *me* and my boys off, is unbelievable.

He is gifted when it comes to the law and funny enough, all the loop holes it has. It bewilders me how clever the fucker truly is. He loves a good argument and the buzz of the ruck, so much so, he would probably argue with his reflection... And win.

He peers over his bifocal lenses at me, as I am brought to the chair beside him.

He gives the plod who brought me up a look, which is one of *'hurry the fuck up and jog on'*, which the plod does, so me and him can talk.

As soon as he does, he turns to me.

"So, what have you said so far?" He has his silver fountain Parker pen at the ready.

"Fuck all," I shrug sitting back with my arms folded insolently. "Cunts have *nothing* on me," he looks at me.

"I do wish you'd stop using profanities when you speak to me." I look him up and down. "What now?" He asks.

"Nothing, just wondering when you chopped your dick off and grew a vagina?" He looks at me shaking his head. *I do like to wind him up.*

"The charges they have, are *very* serious?"

"Aren't they always?" I turn to him. "What do you know?"

"Only what is on the charge sheet, they're grasping at straws if you ask me," he looks at me solidly. "They have NO witnesses..." *They trying to charge me with ABH (actual bodily harm) for Tracie's ex. But it's all circumstantial, they have no evidence.* "Just answer like normal and I'll have you out of here as soon as I can... You have a solid alibi, so let's not worry," he winks.

He signals for them to come in and we get on with the interview. I trust him 100%, hence, why he is here.

I answer '*No Comment*', to *everything*, and I mean everything, even my name.

It's a short interview as expected, they have nothing... *ZERO!!*

I collect my personal belongings from the duty sergeant at the desk, giving him a nasty look as I sign out.

"You're all a bunch of tossers... Why don't you all get real jobs," I yell, giving them a double bird, as I walk out the door with Hammond, who looks very unimpressed at my fond farewell to the boys in blue.

I see Tommy and Big Dave waiting by the Jag for me, as I breathe in the fresh air of freedom.

I say goodbye to Hammond and we pile into the car and are on our way to the club. I'm conscious of the time, so, I know she's still be in the air.

I hate the fact that I couldn't even say goodbye properly, but again, that is how *we* go. *See*, thinking about her again. I can't help myself.

In no time at all, I am sitting at my desk nursing a glass of neat scotch. I hear Tommy knock at the door, I would know his knock anywhere, should do, I've heard it enough over the years to recognise it. I call for him to come in.

He has a worried look on his face and I know he wants to speak about today. Tommy takes the seat in front of my desk, I have my elbows perched on the desk as I look at him.

"What I wanna know Tommy, is, how did the old Bill know where I was?" He shakes his head bewildered.

"Haven't a clue Gov?" He shrugs. "Unless that cunt Jacobs is following you?" He looks at me. "You need to be careful Gov, you know how bad he wants you." I nod, he's right.

"Cheers for calling Hammond," I raise my glass to him, before taking a sip.

"Of course Gov," he purses his lips as he nods. "I knew once you called and told me where you were... It had to be done," I take a glass out of my drawer and pour a drink, sliding it over to him.

"I can always count on you Tommy," he smiles as he raises his glass to salute me, before taking a sip.

I watch him wince at the taste, he's more of a lager drinker. I laugh to myself as I recline back into my leather chair thinking of the times we used to run about the streets as kids, getting up to no good.

I look at him as he tries to continue to drink, but ends up nursing the scotch, pretending he likes it. I often wonder what his life would have been like if he never met me. He is loyal as fuck, always was, never grassed me or no one up. He got the belt from his dad, more than I've had hot dinners, because of me.

My dad didn't really give a fuck, and as for my mum, she fucked off when I was nine. She came waddling back into our lives when I was fourteen, with a half sister.

I was the eldest of three, four if you include my half sister Carly.

Money was always short, tighter though after my mum left.

My dad used to knock her around until one day, she couldn't take it anymore and left. My dad was hardly someone whose footsteps you'd follow. He was a heavy drinker, serial cheater and couldn't hold down a decent job, hence money being so short. I don't blame my mum for leaving, he was a right horrible cunt...

That left me fending for the family. I worked out pretty quickly, the rent needed to be paid after the landlord called round one night and we had to hide behind the sofa. Also food needed to be put on the table, so on and so forth. I found all that responsibility, fell on my young shoulders.

Believe it or not, I liked school, I remember my first day like it was yesterday and how proud my mum was. She took me to the school in my uniform, looking like a proper little good boy. But I weren't...

They were the best years of my life, the innocence of childhood.

But, I was always attracted to doing the wrong thing. My mum reckoned I got them bad genes from me dad. I've lots of his bad habits, I even started smoking at the age of eight, I was a big man, well, I was with the boys in the neighbourhood.

I was the first, not only in my class, but in my local manner, to have the girls interested in me, I always was a player.

That's when the regular canings from the headmaster started. Yeah, you gotta love corporal punishment in schools, I was a product of the reprimanding of the schooling system in the seventies.

I have the gift of the gab, as my mum calls it. It's my Irish blood, which comes from her. Same as my temper. She says I fought to come into this world and no doubt, will fight leaving it.

I'm still the apple of her eye, I can do no wrong.

It was her that got me my first job. A Saturday job, in a butchers, of all places.

Now you know, *how* I got my anatomy knowledge and why I can carve something up without thinking twice about it. I am *still* highly skilled with a blade...

It was handy, as I used to bring home prized cuts for dinner, those that they knew about, and those that they didn't. They took me on full time when I got expelled from secondary school, for smacking a teacher in the face with my fist. However, they did let me go when I got sent to borstal.

That is like a school where your unsocial behaviour and talents are cultivated and perfected by the 'other naughty boys'.

Here, you learnt about life and standing up for yourself. If you didn't, you'd end up being someone's bum-boy. And you can imagine, that kinda thing, *weren't* gonna happen to me.

I had many a fight in there, so for a punishment, the cunts would stop our visits. Fuckers, my mum coming was the one thing I looked forward to. Bless her, she'd bring me fags, which I'd sell, along with the sweets she brought too. I had a good hard name there and one that stood me in good stead for the future.

I still run with some of those nutters, some are 'Faces' themselves now.

Funny, we were well versed when we left there, in the finer criminal arts of intimidation and 'fighting until the death' and being the social rejects we were...

Once I left borstal after my three months, I found life very different. I had a name for myself. The girls love a bad boy and believe me when I tell you. I was a very, very bad boy. I suppose some things never change.

I am quite surprised there isn't millions of mini me's running around the place.

With having to leave school early, I had time on my hands. I was in the football team at school and in borstal. I was good, had talent, could have gone professional. But as with anyone who does sport, you're fucked if you get an injury. That is it, your dream, your life, *is over*. And any boy growing up in the 1980's wanted to be a footballer. That was when the real money started coming into the game for players.

I came from the days where there was no Xboxes or phones, just good, clean fun. Our time was spent outside, running around with a football or on our BMX bikes. Not like the youth of today, who sit as slaves in front of the TV or their video games.

Football was one of the few ways to better of yourself for working-class kids like me. With football, you were either a hunter or the hunted.

I, naturally, was a hunter...

I loved it, football that was, it was my life. I hung around with a crew that were all angry wannabe's like me. They were like me, once the game was over for us all, we turned our talents elsewhere... Like kicking off at the games in the terraces with the rival teams.

That's also the time I first made my acquaintance with Jacobs. He was a street plod then. If I saw him in the riot squad line up, which I did, and often, seeing as the cunt had signed up for that duty. He would *always* be the main focus of my attention. I would take out my frustrations, on Jacobs, for stopping us giving a good hiding to the rival firms.

I, and my like minded friends, looked for trouble and we found it by the truck load. Like in Tottenham in the 1980's, there was the legendary smash-and-grab, at a well-known high street jeweller's. We caused carnage on the streets, there were over 150 thugs arrested that day, none from my firm though. We were far too clever for the old Bill and too fast to catch.

That was the day we realised there was a lot of money to be made out of this. So, it became something that happened regularly, to line our pockets.

We sold all we took, it funded our clothes and trainers and more importantly... Our 'away-game' excursions, to kick the shit out of rival firms and *we* travelled the country far and wide doing it.

We were a solid firm then and I was rising rapidly up the ranks, with a solid rep for being a real HARDMAN.

Then came the *real money* making within the firm. In the 1990's, the UK came alive with dance music and illegal raves. That's where *we* made the serious money and I mean serious.

Point of fact, there is *ALWAYS* money to be made out of drugs, it's easy money...

Our Gov was a clever chappy and always knew a good deal. He saw what I was made of and started grooming me for bigger and better things.

I was always a lucky fucker, being in the right place at the right time...

By the age of twenty four, I had done things people only dreamed of doing... I had stayed in some of the finest hotels, with some of the dirtiest bints you could ever imagine... Drank the finest champagnes and liquors... Taken *most* drugs known to, both man and *horse*. I had money coming out of my ears.

Nothing, however, even comes close, than being in your own firm... *Or...* When it kicks off at a match, and I mean *nothing*. It's a rush, a buzz. I will *always* have that hooligan mentality in me, it makes me, *me*.

I'm classified as a 'Category C risk' with the authorities. I'm not being big-headed, but that is about as high as you can get, for nutters like me. Fuckers could never *actually* pin anything on me though... I *always* came up 'smelling of roses'.

I look at Tommy, he looks tired, I tell him to go home, take the night off, spend some time with his Mrs. don't worry about the celebration party going on downstairs in the club, due to my release.

I'm contemplating doing the same after the party, when I see *'She'* has answered the message I sent earlier...

10

SHAMELESS

I find myself excited at seeing it and eagerly answer. She's giving me one word answers, okay, two words tops. I'm sure it's because of today's events.

Seeing those boys in blue, is *my* world, not '*Hers*'. And, I type like a love sick puppy asking if I can ring her. Surprisingly, she says yes.

"Oi, oi," it's our greeting to each other, done it for years.

"Well hello, I'm surprised you're *out*?"
Bless her, she really don't have a clue about all this legal nonsense.

"Yep, didn't you know... Apparently I'm a good boy," I laugh mockingly. "So, you home?" I pour myself another drink and sit back comfortably in my chair.

"No, I'm on my next job, I'm in a beautiful hotel in China, and I will be for the next week," I hear her move around.

"So, what ya doing?" I find myself trying to imagine what she is doing right now while she is talking to me.

Now, when I do this, I always think of her either stroking her skin as she talks to me or having a good old fashioned rummage, because eventually, that is exactly what *will* happen, with both of us. As I've said before, I've had many a wank after speaking to her and during come to think of it.

"Well, at this moment in time, I am laying on my bed," it looks like the convo is going that way quicker than I thought it would.

Sometimes we do it, like a quick release thing. Bit like a quick fuck.

I would like to ask, if she's eaten anything, I know she didn't have breakfast. But I don't and go straight in for the kill...

"What are you wearing?" I swing my feet up on my desk.

"Actually, I'm wearing the loveliest red satin bra with black lace... My boobs look pretty amazing in it," she laughs. "And of course, I'm wearing the matching panties that go with it. I think you would really like them."

"Your tits would look great in anything... Shame I can't see... Actually, it's a *shame* I'm not *there* ripping them off you." I can feel my cock already getting harder at the thought.

"When you buy me my lingerie, *then,* and only *then*, can you can rip them off me," she laughs."But until *then*, like everything with *us*, you'll have to rely on your imagination... Which is *a shame*," she coo's. "As I could really do with some cock tonight."

Then, she describes what she is going to do to me when she sees me. My cock is so hard, I find myself stroking it through the fabric of my Saville Row suit pants, until I have to release it and start to knock one out. And to look at her, she looks all lady... But her mouth, my God, men would pay good money for her filthy mouth. She would make a fortune with just her talking.

And that's why I spend the next hour on the phone, talking the dirtiest filth to her. I tell her how I am going to make her ride my cock until she screams my name, and I am adamant, that she calls me by my Christian name.

No one calls me by my first name, but I want to hear it purr from her lips as she is cuming. The thought of it alone makes my heart race like a stupid '*loved up*' cunt.

I laugh when she tells me she **won't**. She says she's going to say, '*I'm cuming you cunt!*'. I laugh as I tell her, I don't want that. '*She*' being the minx she is, tells me 'she don't care', she'll call it like it is and that is because... '*I am a cunt*'.

I can't really argue the point seeing as she is right.

That's when I put my cock away. Can't talk all serious with her, with my cock still in my hand.

She also goes on to tell me that she is too good for me... I agree, I tell her I think so too, and that this *fact* has never been in dispute. I know she hates it when I do this, makes her more venomous in her cutting quips.

She then, proceeds to tell me, 'that I don't deserve her'...

I tell her, what I deserve and what I get are two different things altogether. But it don't matter which... *I want her and...* **I will have her**...

She then tells me, that I am only interested in her as I am a hunter. And I only want her, as she must be the only woman I haven't *had*... I tell her she is right... *But I want her **and I will** have her.*

But I do it in my cheeky way. I make her laugh and I mean laugh proper, not with sarcasm. She loves the fact that she gets to see a side of me that only a few people know.

I think she is only one of the few people who do actually understand me and why I am the way I am. I tell her shit that I've never told nobody.

... And I can't help myself, I try to stop myself, but before I know it, I've told her something that I regret telling her. I tell her all amounts of shit, even the birds I'm fucking and what I've done with them. And she listens to it all... Without even batting an eyelid.

I've tried a few times to tell her how I feel about *her*, but she just won't hear it...

Tells me to shut the '*fuck up*', she can't hear that *shit* from me, I need to be all Alpha when talking to her and if I don't, she simply won't talk to me.

ANY, and I mean *any* of my birds *or* bints, would *kill* to be treated the way I treat her, or hear the way I talk with her. *Even my Mrs...*

I've had some lovely girls over the years, but they would only be a close second to '*Her*'. I've lived with a few, but none of them, do, what '*She*' does to me.

See, that is the thing about '*Her*', and being in contact with her. '*She*' changes me, makes me soft in the head and heart. But not my cock... *No*, she has that so *rock hard*, it would be officially classified as a lethal weapon.

She is right! '*She*' really is my kryptonite...

She realises the time and says she has a early meeting so, I reluctantly let her go, telling her I will catch up with her later. And she is gone, leaving me all alone, and with a raging hard on.

I look down and see I am *still* pitching a tent, that could be used happily for a music festival. I pick the office phone up and call down to the bar.

I have a nice bag of coke and Kelly, with the big tits, on her way up, to sort out my cock.

After speaking with '*Her*', I need to get my fuck on and get the cum that has built up again, out of me.

Then I can go downstairs to the celebrations, a happy chappy...

The party really kicks off when I arrive, all my lads are waiting for me, it's like a hero's welcome.

The drugs and drink are flowing like a river. The Lads are snorting off the girls tits and everyone is up for it large tonight. Even though I've had my fill of Kelly, my desires and urges can't be satisfied. With the amount of coke I've done, I will be up fucking all night. So, I decide to take two sorts to the nearest hotel and have myself a nice little threesome.

Even at the hotel, whilst drilling these two sorts and watching the lesbo show they are performing for me, I'm thinking of *'Her'*. The thought of her, is rotting my brain, even with these girls here doing their thing.

This only makes me throw myself into the two wriggling bodies of these girls and enjoy myself, to the point, that their torsos are white with the coke residue from me snorting it off their bodies.

I am out of it, I lie there and let the girls take turns in riding my cock and my face. I couldn't tell you what their names are or what time it is.

But I am still wide awake, as the sun starts cracking through the windows.

The girls are asleep, the sheets wrapped around their naked, bottled tanned torsos.

I'm still doing the odd line or two, I am charged, fuelled by my thoughts.

It's when you're in a drug fuelled haze like this, that your mind naturally goes into overdrive. My anger at yesterday's proceedings, of me getting lifted by the old bill, increase my already heightened state.

I find myself looking at my phone, '*She*' hasn't been online for a good few hours. I know I can't speak to her so '*She*' can calm me down, talk me off my rage ledge. There are some very lucky mother fuckers out there, that are still walking, only due to '*Her*' and her calming influence.

I know I should get some shut eye, but when you have two lovelies in a bed, naked and once you wake them, will be up for anything. I'm sorry, you tell me a man that won't go for some more... And that is exactly what I do as I crawl onto the bed and over one of the girls giving her a poke with my hard cock until she wakes up.

I fuck them both, pretty much most of the morning, until it's check out time. I walk the girls downstairs and even hail a taxi for them.

As they drive off, I call Big Dave, telling him where to pick me up. While I wait for him, I make my way into the restaurant and order a pot of tea .Chatting up the waitress I manage to blag some breakfast for myself, a nice full English with all the trimmings, even though they have stopped serving it

As I am halfway through my food, Big Dave turns up. I motion for him to sit down and order him food too.

He sees I'm antsy, he knows me well enough after a night like I've had, I am still charged, plus, its eating time, which means no talking to me.

But I am also incensed, while waiting for Big Dave, I've seen '*She's*' been online... *AND* she hasn't even looked at my messages. *What the fuck is that all about?*

This just angers me more, to the point I can't even finish my food. This also means poor Big Dave's not going to either, he watches me get up. As I march off I tell him we are heading back to the club.

Little did I know, this would be the start to a very long and shitty week...

We get back to the club and head for my office. It's while I'm taking a call, I hear a commotion going on in the club. I tell them I'll call them back and make my way downstairs.

Waiting for me, is a situation that needs my obvious urgent attention...

Tommy is trying to defuse a very upset Freddie's girlfriend. She is distressed, tears streaming down her face and poor Tommy is trying to do his best in calming her down, but without much success. He is telling her that he hasn't a clue where '*her Freddie is*'.

I can see the look on his face as he is telling her the story that; 'Freddie was seeing one of the waitresses and that a substantial amount of cash was taken by them, the last shift they worked.

She, is having none of it...

Tommy sees me walking to them, she is clueless as her back is to me. He gives me a look, mouthing a '*Sorry Gov*', as I step in.

"What's going on?" I look between the two. "I can hear you upstairs," I look at Freddie's bird. "Look love, we're just not taking on any new dancers... Sorry."

"I'm not here because I want a job!!" She stares at me shocked.

"Oh sorry love, just we get gorgeous girls in here looking for work *every* day," I look at her sincerely. "Sorry if I offended you," I see her face soften slightly. "So how can I help you?"

"I'm Freddie's girlfriend," I look at her, then to Tommy.

"Don't surprise me one bit... Freddie's always had an eye for a stunner," I shake my head. "Where is he?" I look at her. "Your Freddie is in a lot of trouble. I'm sorry to tell you this, but, the ladies weren't the only thing Freddie dipped his hand in, it seems the wages I paid him weren't good enough and he has run off with quite a large amount of money... *Now*, I'm not the kind of person you would steal from. You being here shows me, you know nothing about this. So, I will say to you, if he does contact you... I would suggest telling him that *we will find him*... He can try and hide, but unlike Freddie, I have friends everywhere and it will only be a matter of time until he is caught."

She looks up at me. She knows I mean business and she is reading between the lines as to what I am *actually* saying.

"Freddie wouldn't steal from you," she looks between Tommy and me. "He wouldn't and he wouldn't cheat on me... He just wouldn't. He loves me."

Tommy shakes his head at her as do I. I call one of the waitresses over.

"Daisy, can you tell this young lady who Freddie was friendly with?"

Daisy walks over, shaking her tits and arse as she does. Stopping just in front of Freddie's bird.
She is a typical, stereo typed looking waitress, one that you would expect at a place like this. Her hair is curled perfectly, over made up face like all the girls and has a body that should be made into 'sex doll' mould. She is chewing gum and blowing bubbles, as she looks Freddie's bird up and down.

"Yeah Gov, he was fucking Angel at first... Until Porsche caught his eye... *Fucking bitch* still owes me a tenner. Last time I will lend anyone anything... Her and Freddie were madly in love, he gave her a ring and all... All I can say is that *bitch* will bleed him dry being the bloodsucker she is... I tried to tell him, but you know men." she looks between Tommy and me.

"Sorry Gov, but you men think with the wrong heads... I'd get yourself checked out love," she looks at her. "Freddie boy was a bit of a player," I look at her. "Sorry Gov, just saying, us girls *need* to stick together, she doesn't want a dose or something. I wouldn't let that fucker near me after her, she was a 'dirty bitch whore'."

"All right, all right," I guide her way from the conversation. Thanks Daisy," I shake my head unhappily. "I'm sorry you had to hear all that."

"I don't believe it," the tears are streaming down her face now. "He would never."

I see her go weak at the knees as she crumbles, poor cow, I feel sorry for her, but, needs must and all. *I'm not exactly going to tell her that Freddie is now fish food am I?*

I guide her to a table and sit us down at it.

"I'm sorry you had to hear all that," I purse my lips together. "Unfortunately, in a place like this, and with so many *pretty girls*, things like this happen... He's not the first one, to run off with a woman," I eyeball Tommy and give him a signal, before turning my attention back to her.

"However, what I don't understand, is, when he has someone like *you* to go home to," I look at her. "I mean, seriously, look at you," and I look her in the eye, the drinks that I signalled Tommy for have arrived.

I take the drinks off the tray and place one down in front of her.

"I mean, just look at you... You're beautiful, Freddie was *really* batting above his league with someone like *you*," she sniffs her tears back, nodding her head agreeing with me. "If I was Freddie," I move my hand to hers. "I would finish my shift and rush home to a sort like you, waiting for me at home... I wouldn't be hanging around here *chatting up the girls*."

I shake my head woefully as I take a sip of my drink, knowing full well, if I keep this up, she will follow my lead.

And she does, sipping from her drink casually as I empathise with her situation. *See, always* a chancer.

"Look, I understand, you're upset with Freddie doing a bunk... He's *fucked* us over *too*," I look at her as she nods.

"I don't think he will be brave enough to show his face around here again... I reckon, he's left the country with that tart," I see her lip tremble. "What a prized cunt," I shake my head. "Making a pretty girl like you cry," I signal for another round of drinks, seeing that she has nearly finished hers. "Shame, damn shame, but he ain't worthy of *any* of *your* tears darling."

Believe it or not, but after the second drink, I get Leroy to get her a taxi to take her home, armed with my number... *Just* in case she hears from that cunt Freddie and I tell her if she needs anything, and I mean *anything*, to give me a call. She leaves happy with the story and that should be the end to that state of affairs...

I finish my drink before going back up to my office. On the way I look at my phone, in particular, a social media site and check my messages.

I see she had answered, but it's not the answer I was looking for.

'*She*' tells me that she is tied up work wise and won't be able to message me for a couple of days, but she wants to speak to me. Apparently she is going to a province that doesn't have internet coverage.

I find myself staring at the message, wondering how China don't have coverage, when I remember it's a communist nation and luxuries like the internet aren't available to everyone as it's state governed. Makes you think how lucky we are.

I don't like the fact I can't contact her, like the time when she was married. That's one thing I can't get over, the fact, that she got married.

Never thought I would see the day when that would happen. And I didn't...

I heard about it with second hand information, *after* the event.

I never saw it coming. I thought she would always be untameable, like me, hence why we were so suited to each other.

She has taken over my every thought, it's driving me insane. I'm unfocused which is not like me.

Normally I would either be at home with the Queen Bee, or with some other sort or bint from my harem.

But I find after that little rendezvous in the ladies bathrooms, the need to taste '*Her*', be with '*Her*', is all too consuming.

I'm going to have to sort myself out and sharpish.

I message her back telling her to call me when she is contactable, it's time *we* speak about the future...

I sit there for a while, the coke has got me still charged and after the couple of lines I'm going to do, I will be surging.

My phone rings. It's the dirty bint, she's horny as fuck and wants my cock something bad.

She has a mate over who I've fucked a few times and they want a threesome... Oh happy days.

I needn't tell you, I'm more than happy to go over and lend a helping hand. Her mate is a sort, also likes it up the arse, so having the two of them together will be fun. I call one of the runts to drop some gear around there, a few party treats that should see us right for a few hours, until I get home and take my boy to school.

I'm burning the candle at both ends here I know, but the weekend is coming and so will my come down.

At least I will be able to sleep in, regain some much needed kip and get my head focused.

I do feel a cunt turning the tables on Freddie's girl, but, misdirection is protocol for situations like this.

I arrive at the bints and I'm welcomed in, with open arms and the party begins...

11

BAD HABIT

It's about 6:30am when I leave the bints flat and head for home.

I'm not even the slightest bit tired, I'm still fired up. Mind you, I will say the gear we was snorting, was pretty good stuff, my gear always *is*. And it also helped that the bint and her mate kept me pretty busy with their naughty antics.

Those two are destined to star in a porno one day, and, I'd say, not in the far too distant future either, judging by their performances last night.

If they could have, they would have fucked the cock off me.

By the time I get home, my son is still asleep, so I go and wake him, telling him to come down for some breakfast as usual. Which he does.

It's a normal morning, like any day, I have to nag at him *'to hurry up, we'll be late'*, and so on and so forth. Eventually, we're in the car, heading into London.

My son is playing silly buggers with the radio, wanting to listen to some poxy song. It was only for a moment that I took my eyes off the road...

Stupid cunt in front of me had braked and, I didn't see it... *So...* I rear-end them, crushing their poxy bumper with the solid Jaguars. Of course, they made a scene. A right song and dance about the fucking piece of shit they were driving. I think they took great offense to me calling their rust bucket of a Fiesta Bravo that. But in fairness, it really was.

The old Bill was called, and of course, their fucking ears pricked up when they ran my registration through the system and saw my name pop up. Cunts probably cum in their pants when my name flicked up on that screen. Wankers delayed me big time, I couldn't do shit all about it. You could clearly see it was an accident.

All they could do was to give the dick-head and me our incident numbers, so we could give it to our insurance companies.

That situation made my son late for school. *Now*, he's not a very happy bunny, as he had a school trip.

Yeah, he missed it by an hour. I offered to drive him to the location and meet the trip there, but them snotty cunts wouldn't have any of it. So, you can imagine, that didn't go down too well with him.

And to add insult to his injury, he would have to go into a juniors class. *Yeah*, he is not a happy chappy with his dad.

As I drive back to sort out some personal business I have to deal with, I get a call from Tracie... Apparently her ex had died. His parents have turned off his life support.

Personally, I don't give a shit, I only hope he had a donor card, at least he can be good for something now. But this means, it's now a murder charge.

I give Hammond a call. Thankfully he is aware of the news, he tells me to keep my nose clean, he will find out some more information and call me back.

As I drive back to sort out some personal business I have to deal with.

It's something I do every week, regardless of what is going on in my life... Only a few select people know, including *'Her'*, especially *'Her'*. *'She'* is the major person who is helping me get through this, sort this all out in my head.

After that, I head to the club, I have a few calls and some business to conduct. Out of all my businesses, and I have a good few, I tend to favour the club the most. I spend more time there than the others... Plus, the pussy is on tap.

It's only when I'm there, that I check my phone, just to see if *'She'* has been online. *'She'* hasn't, which pisses me off, even though she has told me that she won't be.

I need to speak to her, I want to off-load my shitty day with *'Her'*, which is something I normally do.

Annoyed with *'Her'*, I call for Kelly to come up to my office.

I hear Kelly knock at the door, I'm just having a couple of lines, to boost me up.

Yeah I know... I'm a cunt.

She walks in and sees me pinching my nose after a snort, wiping off any residue that may still be there.

"Got a line for me?" She flashes a seductive smile as she places her hands on the desk, then leans over enough for me to see her tits housed in her bright pink bra.

"Get your arse round here then," I give her a devious smile, motioning for her to come behind my desk.

She slowly walks round, all the time watching me cut two fat lines for her. I give her a look, motioning with my head for her to grab the rolled fifty pound note.

She's wearing one of those skirts that could pass for a belt.

It's shows off her tanned legs that are housed in six inch slapper heels, a crucial piece of uniform for any girl who wants to earn her money.

She bends over, picks up the note and places it against her nose and hovers over the lines.

Yeah, you know what's going to happen here...

As she snorts her first line, I stroke her folds through her thong. She lets out a '*Mmmmm*', looking back at me before she hovers over the other.

She knows what's coming as she starts to snort, I rip the thong off her. It's not like she is wearing Victoria Secrets and personally, I don't give a fuck if she is either!

I throw them to the floor and place my cock against her opening, as she snorts I plunge deep into her. I tell her to place her hands on the desk and I slam into her, holding her hips to steady her. Pretty soon, the contents on top of my desk are rattling and shaking, as I pound my cock hard into her. She is moaning her '*Mmmm's*' and I'm fucking her frantic.

I am building up a sweat like a race horse, as I feel the cum rise. I slap her arse and pull out. Which is the signal to turn around and drop to her knees and suck me off. She obliges and her mouth is around my helmet quicker than anything, she swallows my load with my hand on the back of her head. I watch as she licks and teases my cock. I line up a few more lines and we continue the party.

Next, I fuck her as she sits on top of my desk facing me, legs spread. She plays with her clit, her fingers swirling. She rubs her hand over her folds and reaches for my cock.

She rubs her cream over my cock as she wanks me, teasing my length. Then she guides it to her opening.

We fuck again, good and hard, enough that a few of the objects on my desk fall to the ground. We hear something smash, but we take no notice as I pound into her.

She keeps trying to kiss me, something I haven't done with her, or many of my bints.

For me, that requires feelings, feelings I don't have for them... *See*, I'm honest.

They know what I'm all about... I'm just surprised that she's trying to make this, something it's not. She tries again, so I put one of my fingers into her mouth, she sucks and teases on that. But I have to give it to the girl, when she tries again. This time, I stop my thrusting, catching my breath.

I know what's coming now...

"Why won't you kiss me?" She tries to look into my face for an answer.

"*Sweetheart*, let's not have this conversation now, *yeah*? Don't rock the boat!"

I disengage from her and put myself back into my suit trousers and zip myself up as I walk away from her, putting some distance between us. She sits there on my desk, obviously offended, which I can understand.

"What do you mean *rock* the boat?" She tilts her head at me. "I thought you *liked* the times we've had?"

"I do... You're a sort," I smile at her. "And you have a lovely pair of tits too... Who wouldn't like you?" I sit down in my leather chair.

She slides off the desk and walks towards me. She spreads her legs either side of mine and she lowers herself slowly onto my lap. I hold her firmly by the hips, knowing full well, what's left of her thong is on the floor. *Yeah, I'm thinking of my suit trousers... Don't want a snail trail do I?*

She, naturally takes great umbrage at this. She tries again to lean in and kiss me, but I hold her firmly and she can clearly see my head turning from hers. She tries again, with the same outcome.

"Why won't you kiss me?" Anger is blazing in her face. "I'm good enough for you to fuck... To suck your cock?" She gets off me, enraged. "Is that all I am? A quick fuck?"

Her head is tilted, her hands perched on her hips, as she stares angrily down at me. I shrug as I shake my head.

This *also* don't go down well either and I have found that I have reached her breaking point. One of the many talents I have perfected over the years with the fairer sex. *You'd think I would learn, but hey, this is **me** we're talking about.*

"Fuck you," she bends to pick up her underwear.

"You did," I purse my lips together looking very smugly. *See*, can't help, but poke the bear, it's the hunter in me.

"You what?" She looks at me astonished with my curt answer, which was exactly what I wanted. "*You fucking what?*" She steps back and looks at me sitting completely composed in my chair. "Did I hear you right?" She cups her ear.

"Yes love, you did."

I look at her briefly, before sitting up and moving my chair to its rightful position at the desk. To add insult to injury, I pick up my mobile and ignore her, pressing the buttons.

Of course, this has the desired effect and the next thing I hear is the door slamming... *Result*!!

After a few calls, I head downstairs, to the death glares of Kelly.

I laugh to myself, if she thinks she'll get any sympathy from the girls, she better think again. They've all been through this, with either me or one of the lads here and a few of the women too.

We're all players here, even the women, with their lady love ways. I've seen straight girls come, work here and at some point, I'm sure their curiosity gets the better of them. Because they always succumb to it. *Plus*, the women here are absolute *vultures*. Always happy to pick up the scraps of the broken hearted... *Me*, personally, I find it quite entertaining, they pick on the weak. *Now you know why I love this club...*

It's my Den... I'm with kindred spirits...My own kind.

Undoubtedly, Kelly's '*wounded*' scent will waft under *their* impatient, always *ravenous* noses and she will get picked apart, like any carcass in the wilderness.

Daisy catches my eye as I walk past her. Her eyebrows raised, asking if it's '*fair game*'. I nod the once, and wonder how long it will take Daisy to taste Kelly. And when I say taste, I mean as in Kelly cuming on Daisy's tongue.

I've seen Daisy in action, shame she loves pussy, she don't '*do*' cock... Unless of course it's a strap-on and she is the one wearing it.

I stand at the bar talking to Tommy and watch Daisy as she goes in for the kill. This kind of thing amuses me greatly.

I see Daisy going to console Kelly, you know, give her a shoulder to lean on. Next will come the drinks, and then a quick joint with God knows what. And before Kelly will know it, Daisy's hand will be stroking her very wet folds and making her cum on her fingers.

I watch, Daisy's 'on form', it's only half an hour when she gives me a saucy wink, as her and Kelly head out to the back.

"See Tommy, that is what I love about this place," he looks at me. "*Animals*, all predatory beasts, *all* converging in one place. This is the ultimate watering hole," he nods to me. I see his face and know something is wrong. "What's up Tommy boy?"

"Just don't think the Kelly thing was a good idea," he sips on his tea.

Bless Tommy, won't have a drink until after 7pm.

Ever since he and his Mrs. knocked out a few rugrats, he sort of behaves himself. He keeps himself busy with the day to day running of this place. Over the years he has become domesticated, more uneasy about getting his hands dirty.

"Why's that Tommy?" I ask, now you see, I'm interested in what he has to say. "Well, seeing you have tits and no balls, maybe you can enlighten me?" He looks at me. "Tommy, I know you're under the wife's thumb and she wears the pants at home... Is that why your siding with some old slapper?" Now he looks hurt. *Okay, maybe a step too far.* "Look Tommy," I put my arm around his shoulder. "She's fallen for it," and I grab my cock through my trousers. "She wants more of this, and unfortunately, due to my roguish charms, she wants this?" And I point to my heart. "Now you know and I know... That's not on the cards for her," I drop my arm off his shoulder, my advisory duties ceased. "She knows the score," and I turn and peruse the comings and goings of the staff, on their way.

"I know Gov, but you should have seen her when she came down after, she looked like she was spitting venom."

"She probably *was,* with that tongue," I laugh.

"Gov, you know it's not good having a angry girl here," he looks at me sincerely.

He has a point.

"And now *Daisy*," he rolls his eyes. He knows Daisy is a huge lesbo slut, she is like me, but a woman. "If Kelly finds out," he shakes his head woefully.

"And how will she find out?" I look at him. "You going to tell her when you two are changing your Tampons?" I glare at him. "Do me a favour, *fuck off* and *grow some* will you?" I look at him with distain. "Seriously Tommy, what the *fuck* has happened to you mate, you're pussy whipped?"

I can't even look at him, I walk away, the need to thump him in his face has become all too much. I mutter to myself 'Pussy whipped *cunt'*. I don't give a fuck if he hears me and wants to go and cry in the girls toilets. *Wanker*!

I go to head back up to my office, to the coke, to be more precise.

Also, I'm gonna call Queen Bee and tell her to pick the boy up from school, I'm too charged and fucked off. That's when I hear a familiar voice.

"*Well*, *well*, if it ain't the *main man* himself," it's Tony Boyle, affectionately called 'Mad Dog'.

He was here the other night attending the big meeting, a right lary fucker, hard as nails.

I think he should be called Rabid Dog, as that is exactly what the fucker is like, when he goes off on one. He, like myself, has rep. Rose up through the ranks like me. But that is where the parallels end.

This cunt, will fuck anything with a heartbeat, and I mean anything, even his cell mate whether he wants to or not. *Yeah, now you get my drift.*

Has *NO CLASS* whatsoever. But in fairness, he *is* from north of the River Thames.

"North London," I turn around and walk to meet him and his two pit-bull looking mother fuckers. "I shit em," I laugh as I extend my hand in a friendly shake. "What brings you *this side* of the river?"

See, what I'm doing here now, is clearly *and* nicely, pointing out that *he is in fact, on my turf.* Believe it or not, this is a polite greeting.

"Just seeing if it's true, that the tossers here, are wanking each other off seeing you're all cocksuckers and all," he laughs.

"Drink?" I motion to the bar.

"Don't mind if I do, how very civilised of you," he mimics the gentry, as we walk.

I see his two pit-bulls are lagging behind, I also clock Leroy and Ellis. They happen to be fucking huge and very intimidating looking 'Geezers' who just turn out to be head of my security here at the club.

Leroy and Ellis come from the old days too, pure muscle and very game to give anyone a good kicking without even thinking about it. 'Mad Dog's' two pit-bulls, are no match for even one of them.

Our drinks are served and we partake in some idle chit chat.

"So, what brings you back so soon to my gaff?" I sip on my scotch as I watch him almost neck his, in one gulp.

"My sisters *dozy bollocks of a fella*, has gone walkabout," he looks at the barmaid and signals for her to refill his glass again.

"What's that got to do with me?" I look to him. "You reckon he's come *this* side of the water?" I finish mine and the glass is refilled.

"He was a barman here," I nod. "My sister Krissy, was in the other day."

The penny drops... Freddie's bird is '*Tony Boyles', fucking* **sister**??

"Are you telling me that *thieving cunt* is from your firm?" I look at him menacingly. "You doing so bad you have to get one of yours in, to steal from me?" I glare into his face.

"He's *NOT fucking* with *US*?" He says with distain. "He couldn't fight his way out of a wet paper bag... Can't stand the worthless cunt personally. He's a *fucking* wrong-un, always was," he signals for his glass to be refilled. "*But*, she *loves the mug*."

The barmaid looks to me, I nod as she comes with the bottle. 'Mad Dog', grabs it out of her hand.

She looks to me and I motion its cool, she backs away from us. I know Leroy and Ellis are alerted too. They see fucking everything, perfect guys to have watching your back.

No fucker would ever get through them. I watch as 'Mad Dog' pours himself another drink and refills mine too.

"Nice place you have here," he gulps his drink in one and refills it again.

Oh, I need to tell you, drink and drugs actually don't go very well with Tony, sends him loopy, hence his name, 'Mad Dog'.

"*So*," coolly, I take a drink and place my glass down on the bar. "*No* need for *me* or *my boys* to *look* around *your way* for him then? Seeing as *you're here* on **my manor**," he nods as he pours another drink for himself. *Now*, I need to style it out, keep up appearances, flexing my muscles, figuratively speaking.

"Yeah, I suppose not," his face grimaces.

"*Still*... There *is* the small matter of the money that he took when running off with that slapper."

"Nothing to do with me **or** my little sister," he looks at me. "She said you were nice to her the other day."

"You know me Tony," I laugh. "I'm always *nice* to the ladies."

"Not my baby sister you're not, you cunt," he turns to me, his face snarling. "You keep your dirty paws off her... I know what you're like."

"Talking of which... How is your mum?" I look up at him smirking. "Would be nice to see her again... I'll get some condoms for doing her this time, seeing as she'll ride anything, even ya fucking leg."

See, pure hunter, always up for it.

Naturally, with something like this, being said to you, about your dear ole mum... It kicks off.

Yeah I know, I have huge balls, but who does the fucker think he is? Bringing two cunts around to my gaff and drinking yourself up some courage so you can feel brave enough to have a go... Fuck yeah... Game on.

And in a blink of an eye, I see 'Mad Dog's' fist, come hurtling towards my face...

Cunt is too slow, he's not disciplined like me.

His free time is spent down his local boozer, training his drinking arm if you get my drift. *Me*... I train five to six days a week at the gym.

Fucker don't stand a chance, as I dodge it and nut him straight, full force, in the face... And the fuckers nose bursts open. I take my chance to land a series of heavy punches to his stomach and kidneys.

Leroy and Ellis are on *his* boys like lightening and are knocking six bells of shit out of them. Tony is holding out his hands in front of him, trying to catch his breath. It seems I knocked the wind out of him with the blow to the stomach. It don't help him much, what with claret all over his face and somehow, the soppy cunt has got it in his eyes, blinding him.

I see my chance and take the fucker out with a few more blows, couple more to the stomach, seeing as its weak and vulnerable. That's the lion in me. And a perfectly placed 'upper-cut' to the jaw, even if I do say so myself. It must have hurt, as he spits out a few teeth, and his jaw is hanging limply, no doubt like his flabby cock.

Tony falls to his knees.

I see a chance, with one foot, I bring it swiftly up, as though I am scoring the *winning goal*.

It's as my foot makes contact with his balls, that he lets out this terribly girly scream, when Big Dave enters swiftly to the commotion.

He mouths a '*Sorry Gov*' as he scrapes 'Mad Dog' off the floor, who's now clutching his vagina. He assists Leroy and Ellis with ejecting our 'uninvited guests' from my establishment.

I am feeling a million dollars, unstoppable, with the adrenaline coursing through me. That, and the *coke* I had earlier.

I turn to see Tommy standing at the foot of the stairs. He is shaking his head and has a worried look on his face.

Even though 'Mad Dog' came in here, giving all the 'big-un', *and* threw the first punch...

It is me... I'm the one...

I, have just affirmed... An *all out* **war**, between *our Firms*...

12

AROUND TOWN

By 7pm, my club is full, with *MY Firm*. The atmosphere is electric, hooligans, thieves and thugs, wall to wall... My men...

I made a few calls, put the word out that; '*War was upon us*'...

Its rowdy, as one would expect, no punters in here tonight. Just my crew of social degenerates, fuelled with the best drugs and filled to the gullets with booze.

They are pure animals... **My animals***...*

These boys will blow a place apart, in the blink of an eye. We have even travelled the country kicking the 'ever living shit' out of other firms.

These are the men to go into war with, to have standing by your side. We are solid.

I get up on the stage, it's a party atmosphere, things have been too quiet and civilised between the firms for far too long now. They have been itching for a barney for a good while. I needn't tell you, I was already the *'Lord and Master'* before my meet with 'Mad Dog'... *Now, now I am a Legend... I am a God...*

I was before, but now, *my name*, will forever be synonymous with today's happening and its future outcome, My name be written in the book of legends, all good with me.

I know them North London cunts will come at us with everything they have. All due respect to them, they have a great name for themselves, have done for years and years. They are proper hard bastards, they bring fear to other firms, but not us...

They are the only ones who could match *us* with rep. So, by rights, it had to be done. Always has to be a 'Top Firm', and I know *mine,* is it.

I've sat at the head of the table for long enough, time *they* knew it too. 'Mad Dog' knew what he was doing when he walked into my club, coming this side of the river, uninvited and all.

Now, don't get me wrong, I'm not putting them down, quite the contrary. They have been run by 'brains' for years.

They make shit loads of money due to it.
But they lack the muscle power like I have.

Me on the other hand, as you can tell, I have
not only the brains and the brawn, but I have the
looks too. *Yeah, I am a cocky cunt.*

*Thing is, I'm not even from this part of town.
But make no mistake... I fucking run it...*

I give them a pep talk, rattling their cages,
fitting seeing as most of them should be locked up
in one. I come off the stage to roars of battle. These
boys want it, as bad as me.

I nod to Leroy to let the girls come in. They
do, bare tits and all, carrying bowls of coke and
pills. Lads are going to get good and proper fucked
up tonight...

This weekend, we go to war, this could be
our last... And it very well could be, knowing the
North London firm.

They will be coming tooled up, *blood will
be shed...* This we know. They will hit us hard.

All that needs to be decided is where the
battleground will be? That will be something that
their Governor and me will decide.

But make no mistake, this battle *WILL* commence and *this* weekend. Matters like this are dealt with as swiftly as the charges, we will be making at each other.

If you've ever seen a major fight, believe me when I tell you, it is like combat. You are charged at, they come armed with weapons that, if they don't kill you, they will put you in the hospital for a good while. You know they are the enemy. there is no love or respect, just hatred, you want blood. You won't give a fuck how you will get it either. You go into this euphoric state of being a fighting machine. You feel invincible, your brothers by your side, raging to go… And the rush of when you charge at them. Make contact with their bodies and skulls, its animalistic, primal and we are savages.

We are comrades, we come, we devour and tear up anything in our way... Other firms, the old Bill... Don't matter, we will have you and spit you out when we are done with you.

The evening rolls on, everyone wants to talk to me, be seen with me. The party is at its full force, all I can see is naughty antics going on.

Snorting, pill popping like they were 'm&m's. Blow jobs, lap dances, you name it.

It's a proper 'Den of iniquity'...

*Bet your wondering what the name of my club is by now? **'Iniquity'** of course! Only right... It's fitting don't you think?*

I'm watching the carryings-on with Tommy and a few of my 'Head Faces', from the balcony on the sweeping staircase.

I study my army, because, let's face it. That is exactly what they are.

We talk over battle strategies, who will go where and all that.

What, you think I would let my lads run blind, like idiots into North London? They would get cut to bits in seconds.

Understand, this ain't like those poxy films you see on the telly. *Fuck no*, it's real and so are the wounds.

Any general who thinks he can send his troops in, unprepared, is a *cunt* who shouldn't be in the position he is in. As I said, blood will be spilled, I just don't want it being my lads' blood.

We take our meeting up to my office, that way, we can mull over things and have a few lines too while we're at it.

That night, when the meetings finish, I head over to the dirty bints. I am charged like the fucking Duracell bunny, ready to go.

And she is too, she opens the door, a saucy smile on her face as she pulls it open for me to walk in.

She's just closed it, when I'm on her mouth and as usual, until she is on her knees sucking me off.

This is the life... And I am living it large.

To my surprise I wake up with the bints arm draped across my chest. I don't normally sleep here, only fuck. I get up, leaving the bint still asleep and get dressed. I throw some money down and leave like I always do.

However, once back in the comfort of my car, that Big Dave dropped off, I get to thinking that I've seen this bint quite a few times already this week. Gonna have to sort that one out too.

I look at the phone I've place into the charging unit. Unbeknown to me, my battery died at some point last night. Also it dawns on me that I've not thought about '*Her*' until now. *See*, this is the side of me I don't like. I want to think about nothing but her.

I have a lot going on this week… I need to get my head into gear.

I have a big deal going on that will be my golden ticket out of here. And if the weekend pans out like its planned... I will be departing with a '*God Like*' status, along with it.

I look at my phone and see '*She*' has responded to my messages. Apparently I sent a good few last night. Now I know why my battery died. I was too fucked-up to notice at the time. And judging by my messages, I was totally mashed.

It seems… I was *so invincible* last night, I told her exactly what I wanted... *Yeah, in loads of messages* apparently. I'm actually laughing at myself, cringing ever so slightly at some. *Wow*, I would pull the piss out of any of my lads if I knew they had done this.

Good job, I'm more of a 'do as I say', rather than a 'do what I do' type of bloke.

Eventually I get to '*Her*' response, my heart is banging in my chest with anticipation...

'Okay, *HARDMAN*, I see you're putting your cards on the table... But, I do think twenty messages is a bit much though, you melt. It seems though, we DO need to talk...'

I imagine *'Her'* saying HARDMAN, *my name*... Instantly my cock stirs...

It seems my chap, is as smitten with *'Her'*, as I am, even though I give him an array of beauties. Like me, its *'Her'* we want. And apparently... I told her this last night.

Last night, it seems I not only created war...

I also declared my undying love for this woman too...

Personally, I'm pleased with her answer, as I pull off and go about my business.

The day goes quick enough. I visit most of my business outlets, show my face, do what needs to be done. I head to the gym and pull on some weights, then have half hour in the steam room. I need to get all the drug shit out of my system from last night. After, I go for a swim and then hit the sauna.

Following the gym I head home and spend some time with my boy. The Queen Bee is nagging, enough that I tell her *'fuck this for shit,* as I walk out and into my car, heading for the club.

Back at the club, things have relatively, returned to normal.

I have some lads there, just in case anyone gets lary before kick-off and fancies a go.

Now you're probably wondering about this murder charge and has it all magically disappeared?
Answer... No... Of course its fucking not? But it will be...

I know Jacobs and his wankers are sniffing around my arse so much, that I'm surprised I haven't shit on their noses.

But they have *nothing* on me. I'm keeping away from Tracie, she knows the score with something like this. Plus, Steph, the princess of my harem is my alibi. They have video of that wanker going through lights in his boy-racer car, clocking 95mph in an 60mph zone at 00:24, and I was clearly at hers, even the pizza delivery guy remembers me complaining about the 'no ice cream' she wanted.

Yeah, he is one of my runt dealers, but kosher with the proper job of pizza boy.

He just delivers *my desserts and treats* when ordered by his regulars. He is small time really, but he knows he will be looked after for doing me a good turn.

So, I'm not too worried about them being honest... *But*... Jacobs has a nose for all things *me*, and he is desperate to collar me real bad.

He's like a fucking Jack Russell, cunt never lets go and he's a yappy fucker too.

As for the bats that were used... *Yeah*, they got burnt, now just ashes, no DNA, seeing as it's been scattered into the wind.

So *no*, I'm not too worried...

What I am worried about, is speaking to '*Her*'. I really put my cards on the table, proper like. There is no going back, and being honest, I don't want to. After all of these years, I see the prize right in front of me, its reachable... '*Her*'.

I'm more than happy to walk away from all of this... I know '*She*' is worth it... I only wished I had realised this all those years ago in the toilets of my local. That night, would have changed everything for me.

I have everything planned out in my head, being honest, I've already kicked some of this off. Like where I will go and how exactly I will get there.

That bit is easy. I have a friend with a helicopter who is more than happy to pick us up at an old airfield and fly us over to France.

I have friends there too and transportation by water, from a captain friend of mine who owes me a favour or three, to take us to the villa I have secretly bought.

I plan on having a very comfortable life with *'Her'*. The thought of it alone fills me with these stupid gooey feelings I'm really not used to... But, strangely... *I like it...*

The big deal is happening tomorrow. Everyone knows what needs to be done. Let's just say for the moment, it involves a high powered speedboat, under the dark of night, carrying a very large shipment of party favours.

It carries a maximum sentence to anyone caught with their hands on the cookies and no one wants to spend that amount of time staying at 'Her Majesties Pleasure'. It's a serious amount of time, so things have to be run with military precision at both ends. Too much money riding on this for anything to go wrong.

I find myself up in my office, checking the poxy time in China. I want to get all my ducks in a row...

As you've probably gathered, I'm a master planner, in all things.

This is the cherry on the cake for me. I'm looking forward to speaking to her. I need to hear *'Her'* voice. I need to sort *US,* for once and for all. Lots has happened since *'She'* went and its only been a few days.

My life truly is mad...

I know she will hit the roof when she finds out what I've done, and what is planned for the weekend, she will blow a fuse at me.

As I've said, *'She'* really doesn't like *all this nonsense,* so, it should make for good conversation, *once* we've discussed all other matters...

... And yes I will tell her *everything.* I always do, *no matter* what it is.

But I will make sure I won't tell *'Her'* all this shit until after, the important *'Her'* and me talk.

And there was me thinking this was going to be a bad week...

13

AKA WHAT A LIFE

I'm uneasy throughout the night, knowing tomorrow, my deal of a lifetime is happening.

The shipment is coming in and at some point in the morning I will receive possession, of said shipment and sort the lads out for their trouble quite handsomely.

I'm also waiting to hear from '*Her*' to let me know when it's okay for her to speak. *I fucking hate waiting as you can gather.*

I've passed Kelly on to Daisy and my cock needs tending to. *So...* I pick up the phone and call my favourite dirty bint.

I want her to talk dirty to me, and bless her, *she tries*, but she's more of a *doer*, if you get my drift. I literally spend five minutes talking to her before hanging up.

I go down to the club, see who's there. I'm feeling naughty, I'm looking for someone to join in with my antics.

I spy Daisy still laying it on thick with Kelly. My curiosity is spiked and I want to know if she has bagged her yet? So, I make my way over to the bar.

I give Daisy a devilish look, she knows it all too well, we've been doing this for a while now. She give me a impish smile of pure and utter deviancy. Now I know she has banged the fuck out of her.

I call her over to have a drink with me. I know all too well, she will be happy enough to tell me exactly what she has done with her. So we sit in my booth and have a couple of drinks while she tells me all the gory details. The club starts to get busier and duty calls, always money first, so I send Daisy back behind the bar.

It's only moments after that, my message tone of the phone beeps.

I take it out of my breast pocket to see '*Her*' name. Smiling to myself I head up the stairs and back to my office.

I dial her number and wait like a muppet for her to answer. As she does, I throw my feet up on the desk and sit back and relax.

"Oi, oi," I banter. "How are ya?"

"I'm good thanks," she laughs. It's good to hear her voice, it immediately calms me. "*So*... I take it, you're fully recovered from the other night then?" You can hear the sarcasm ooze from her, but I love it.

"I am," I laugh, she is such a cheeky bitch. "So, how is work?"

"So and so," I hear her dragging on her cigarette before exhaling.

'*She*' really is playing it cool, mind you I'm not surprised seeing as I did overdo it a tad on the old messages the other night.

And knowing her, she's not going to beat around the bush and she will get straight to the point.

"*So*… The other night," she pauses momentarily. "What was that *all* about? And before you answer, remember what I have said to you previously about getting all mushy on me."

See, Lioness, goes straight in for the kill, no fucking about.

Now I'm wishing I *had* done a line or two, before I made the call. She would go nuts if I did one now, she don't tolerate that kind of shit. No matter how sneakily I would try to do it. I take a deep breath and talk.

"Okay… We've known each other for a long time yeah?" I hear her agree with me and I continue. "Well, what I said in the messages…"

It's at this point I realise how them pleading fuckers who try to talk and only their lips move, feel. I'm choking here on my own words…

I'm feeling vulnerable, something I am not used to feeling. I look at my desk drawer knowing full well I can have myself some Dutch courage with a few lines… *You know, grease the wheels*.

Instead, I reach for the bottle of scotch and a glass and pour myself a large drink.

"Yes and? I mean, where did it come from? Were you on some mental bender or something?" She laughs, clearly taunting me.

See, plays me at my own game, she's definitely right about the kryptonite thing.

"Something like that... It's been nuts here since you've been gone... Lots has happened."

"Well, that's coz, you is busy innit," she laughs going all urban and all. Her linguistical talents really hold no bounds.

"You don't know the half of it," I laugh thinking to myself, '*she will do later*'. "So, I meant what I said, let's go... I have the ideal place where we can hole up for a while." There is a long silence, well it seems it to me, until she responds.

"And what about work?" She is clearly shocked.

"I'm done... I'll walk away from it all... With *YOU*."

"With me? *Hmmmmm*... Until you get bored or your cock sees something you like... Don't make me laugh," she scoffs. "And what about Rita?"

"Rita… What's she got to do with it?" If I was on a normal phone, I'm sure I would be staring into it now.

"Well considering she *is* Connor's mum, I think *everything*… I mean, it's not like you're going to walk away from him now are you?"

"There will be readjustments for everyone for a little while, until a permanent arrangement can be made… Look, Connor isn't going to be an issue."

"The work thing is though Hardman… Always was."

"I'm telling you… I'm *done*, I've enough money to set myself up very nicely and live like a king… I want you to be my Queen, I want the ring, the works… You know I've not said that to anyone else" *God, I'm so smooth*, I can hear her thinking over our silence.

"Until the next Queen in-waiting comes along," she laughs mockingly. "You know what they say don't you *Hardman*… A mistress who becomes a wife… Only leaves a vacancy for another mistress."

Boom, see that for a kick in the nuts. It's the way she thinks that intrigues me so much, she has an answer for everything.

"Not fair, I'm laying it out on the line here… You know how I feel," she don't even let me finish.

"Yes, with your hands… And they have a tendency to wander… Which brings me to the point of your other tarts… What are you going to do about them?" She sighs heavily. "Look, we need time to talk about this more."

"Well… I've got all night…" I take a drink, smiling to myself. "Look, I'm being serious… *YOU*, you have crawled into my head," I feel my hand go to my temple as I speak. "I can't get you out of my nut… It's you, always has been, we've always had something."

"Yes… Bad timing," she scoffs.

"Yeah that too… But *now* is the time… Look, when are you back in the UK?"

See, sounding needy again aren't I? But I don't give a fuck.

"Look, you know we are meant to be together… You know it… I know it… Let's stop fucking around… I want you… I want you like I've never wanted anyone in my life."

"Yeah right," she laughs. "That is only until you have me... Then something else will catch your eye… You can't help it… You're a hunter, a predator… It's a natural thing for you… You're not for caging… Okay, well you should be… In a prison cell," she mocks. "You're not for taming Hardman... You're *wild*."

"You can tame me," I chirp up as I wince to myself, *what a muppet I am.*

"*Hardman,*" she laughs. "The only whips and chains you should see, should be that of a sexual nature, and personally… I'd like your hands to be free," she purrs.

See, see what she's done there? She's turning '*this*' into a rummage session, like normal. She is hoping I will fall for her trap and deviate from our topic.

"Don't change the subject," I try to contain the laughter. "I'm being serious here," I shake my head.

I really don't understand why she won't talk to me... I know how she feels about me. I felt it in her kiss... She had her eyes shut, for fucks sake and we all know what that means, don't we?

"I just don't think you've thought this through."

"Believe me when I tell you... I've thought about nothing else... Have done for a number of years," she is silent, contemplating what to say next.

"*Years?*" She questions me. "Exactly how many years?" I see her curiosity is sparked with my statement.

So... I'm going to hit her with the truth, seeing, that's what we do.

"Three years ago, when you crawled into my nut and took up permanent residence there... So... roughly, about the time we started sharing... But the truth is... It has to be that night... *All* them years ago... When I looked into your eyes... I saw the future... I saw *my* future."

I hear '*Her*' gasp in astonishment. She wasn't expecting me to hit her with that. But it's true, that's how I feel.

"Look, we should do this face to face... I know I'm asking you to take a gamble... A huge one, but it's not really if you think about it?"

"How do you work that one out then Hardman... This, I've got to hear?" She laughs.

"Well, it's *me* taking the big gamble if you think about it," I hear her scoff. "No seriously, hear me out... You're divorced."

"Wow... Shit Hardman, nice... So, because I'm divorced, my life doesn't *matter*?" She is spitting feathers, but in fairness, she did interrupt me.

"No," I laugh. "You know that's not what I meant, shit. Who rattled your cage?"

"You did, as usual," I hear her light another cigarette and snap her lighter shut.

"What I meant was, that you're as free as a bird, no commitments, not like me, as you know... My life ain't exactly the norm," I find myself speaking quickly, like a used car salesman. How can I not, my life is so messy.

"Well, it would be, being the sultan of a harem," she coos, mocking me.

"I'm serious, I want you... You know I do," I purr down the phone. "Told you, I am walking, I want you at my side."

There is silence, I know she is taking in everything I am saying.

"But for how long?" She sighs. "I just can't see you walking away from it all, especially Connor... I know he means the world to you... And Rita," she sighs again, this time it's heavier. "I feel sorry for her, I really do... Does she even have a clue as to what is going on with you two? Does she even have any idea *this* is coming her way?"

"Things haven't been right between us in years... You know I am only there for my boy... That's why I," I hesitate as I am going to be cringing. "Why I have the others," I can't even say women.

See, see what I mean. I was fine with my life until she crawled into my head. "You know this already."

" Still Hardman, she is Connor's mum, you need to work out custody? You can't take a child away from his mum... And you said something about a villa? Can you really see yourself only seeing Connor for holidays? You can't take the boy away from his mum... I can't be party to something like that, nor will I."

"We can sort something out, all I know is that I have to get out of this and soon," I pour myself another glassful.

"I don't know, this is all a bit too much," I hear her laughing. "Man, I knew I was a good kisser, but this is an actual record for me," she chuckles again.

I know her enough to recognise this as '*Her*' nervous laugh. I need to get in and reinforce my intentions.

"Look, I know with my track record you're nervous... It's understandable. But believe me, you can go at anytime, it's not like I have a gun held at your head," I laugh. "Look, you know we get *on*, I know it, you know it. You know we would be good together."

"I dunno Hardman, I mean, we've only kissed."

"Yeah, bet you haven't thought about anything else since? I know I haven't... I got a taste for you something bad... I knew it would be fireworks and it was, wasn't it... I know you felt it too, so don't bullshit me *Harlow*!"

"I, *Errmm*, I," '*She*' is lost for words.

"When are you back?"

"Tuesday," she's still shocked, I can hear it.

"Send me your flight times and I'll pick you up? We can talk things over... *Yes*?" I know she is mulling it over.

"The airport?" '*She*' laughs. "What if you get lifted there again, seeing as there is a strong police presence there? I don't want to be with you then, if that happens," she chuckles. "Maybe it's best if I meet you in London?"

"God," I laugh. "Anyone would think you don't want to be seen with me?"

"I don't," '*She*' laughs.

"Wow, kick a man while he's down, why don't you?" I banter.

"Yeah... *As if* anyone would have you down... You is the *Hardman*, innit... Hardman by name, Hardman by nature," she teases.

See, she strokes my ego, always has. She said the same thing to me the night I walked her home... *Yeah*, the one I didn't even get a snog for. But she does it for me 'big time'.

"So, you don't want me to pick you up then?" I tease.

"Nope, I'll make my own way... So, tell me what's been going on with you, since I left your whoring arse behind in London?"

I then go on to hint to her that I have business to conduct tomorrow... Means when we leave, we go with so much money I could never actually count it all. '*She*' laughs, asking will I actually bring a bag like they do in the films. I do have a good giggle at this and tell her, yeah, I will have a bag of money I will carry, to a certain extent, however, large quantities of money like that amount, are normally held in Swiss bank accounts for people like me ...

I also tell her that '*She*' will have access to these accounts, I will sort out the paperwork. I needn't tell you, that statement alone blew her away. '*She*' can't get over how much I trust her.

See, '*She*' has them trust issues, has them walls, which I make crumble when I do things like that.
We end up finishing the conversation, with '*Her*' agreeing to meet me in a hotel on Tuesday when her flight lands.

Just in time for a knock at the door, I know it's Tommy, so I tell him to 'come in'. He comes in and I see worry written all over his boat.

"What's up Tommy boy?" I smile, feeling on top of the world. "Shipment come in yet?"

"On its way Gov from what I understand," he shuffles in and sits down in the chair in front of my desk.

"So why the face like a slapped arse?" I chirp.

"I'm worried about this kick off on Saturday Gov," and he is, I can see it written all over his boat.

"Don't be, I sip casually with an air of confidence. "It's all in hand Tommy."

"I've had word, that if you win on Saturday, they are sending someone in for you," I see him dragging his bottom lip through his teeth. It's his nervous tick thing he does, always has.

"*I see,*" I scoff as I take another mouthful of the tawny liquid and let it slide down my throat, reclining back into my chair. "*Fuck it*, I expected as much. Wankers, can't even take the beating we're gonna give em," I shake my head. "Fucking pussies."

"Gov," he shakes his head. "A 'Hitman'?" Again, he shakes his head woefully. His eyes are fearful.

"Tommy, it is what it is," I shrug. "But I'll be ready for them. Remember... Knowledge is power Tommy, never forget that," and I tap my temple to enforce it. "Now I know that privy bit of information, I will be on my guard," I take another drink, a smug smile on my face. "We're going to go in early and hit them at their local... I want their manor obliterated, no one left standing. *Cunts*, won't know what's hit them," I laugh.

I feel...

Untouchable...

Omnipotent...

14

STAKE A CLAIM

It's Friday... The deal is done, the money is in the bank, now all that has to be done, is the gear to be shifted which won't be a problem.

Being the business head I am, I've already set up the deals. I should have the majority of the monies being transferred into my Swiss account by Tuesday, for when '*She*' gets back; *Result*.

And Jacobs and his wankers are clueless as to my other activities. He's too busy trying to get people to turn over on me and squeal. But, unlike Jacobs and his tossers...

I'm liked and more respected in my manor than the old Bill. *So, good luck there Jacobs.*

Me, being me, I've made a few calls, rallying the troops.

I've told them to meet up at our local. I can't have all that mob in here, it's a Friday and there is too much money to be made from normal Friday trade. Too much for me to close my gaff for them animals.

So late afternoon I, Big Dave and a few lads take a drive down for a meeting.

We get there and the lager is plentiful, along with a few recreational substances too. Everyone is in great spirits. We walk into the bar, to the terrace chants bellowing out from their mouths. *Yeah*, these animals are up for it big time. I run through the plans for tomorrow.

They, like me, love the fact, the other 'Firm', will be off their guard. They are expecting a civilised rumble at our preordained location. They really won't know what's hit them, when we come for them.

Me and my lot, spend an hour or so there, chatting and giving pep talks before we head back to the club.

Tommy has Big Dave shadowing me, ever since he got the tip off about the hit. Even if I go to the bog, he's by my side. I laugh to myself, thinking of the poor cunts having to go through Big Dave, just to get to me.

Yeah, you could say I am feeling pretty on '*Top of the World*' at the moment...

Everything is going to plan. All we need, is the morning to come and we are going to smash the hell out of their manor.

After a few hours of being at the club, and one of those spent talking to '*Her*'. I head off to Steph's.

I'm greeted like a king, she is more than happy to see me, so much so, that she is sucking on my cock, good and proper. She has me pushed up against the wall and she's on her knees. It's the perfect start.

Pretty soon we head upstairs and we take full advantage of every surface. I drill her every which way I can, until my cum is completely depleted.

I actually have a sound sleep, I'm not worried about tomorrow.

I know what my firm is made of. These lads will stand their ground and battle through anything... And I mean *anything*.

I shower, go down for breakfast and once finished, I leave.

I walk out her door to be met by the sight of Big Dave, talking to Ellis, beside the Range Rover.

They immediately notice me and nod in acknowledgement , which I return and we pile into the car. We make our way through the London traffic, over to *their* side of the river... In particular, two streets away from their local, which is their meet up point.

Our firm converges together, all you hear are footsteps. No chanting as we walk shoulder to shoulder. I would say an aerial view of this would be quite spectacular to see. There are about two-hundred plus of us descending on them, and they haven't a fucking clue it's about to happen...

But they will, when the poncy benches they have outside, come smashing through their windows...

I watch it happen, as my firm start bowling simultaneously through the three doors they have into this shithole.

It is chaos... Pure and utter pandemonium is breaking out. People are running at each other clashing, swinging clubs and bats. We took them by surprise.

It's violent, menacing, aggressive, obscene and confrontational behaviour, with individuals fighting hard amongst themselves. I hear bottles and glasses being smashed. I know they are being used as weapons due to the obvious cries of pain that come with it... Same as the bar stools, as they are smashed against bodies until they break... They are still useful as weapons, the legs being used as koshes. It's carnage, plain and simple, and in a confined place. All you can hear are the thuds of bedlam, along with metal bars and wood against bodies.

I see 'Mad Dog', and he me, as he tries to make his way over the sea of scuffling bodies to get to me. Just as he does, fucker starts glaring at me like a cunt, yelling like a fucking mental Viking... He was giving the 'large-un' so much, he didn't see Big Dave's fist knock his jaw off its hinges. *Cunt*, quite rightly, hit the deck.

Fuck him, I step over him as he rolls, dazed on the floor. I'm working my way through the crowd, punching and stomping as I go.

I'm hitting some of them fuckers so hard, they'll have lumps on them forever, that's if I haven't cracked their thick skulls or bones already.

We really are tearing this place apart, good and proper. There isn't a window or furnishing left untouched... Next thing we know, some *cunt* has let a CS gas canister off, in the obliterated pub.

The air is so thick with it, we can't breathe, let alone see. So we all make our way out onto the street, still fighting tooth and nail.

It's a fucking great ruck, fists are flying, the adrenaline is pumping through everyone... We are all high on violence and we love it...

We hear sirens and see the blue flashing lights, signaling that our time here is up and we all scarper our separate ways. Of course, I'm flanked constantly by my shadows, Big Dave and Ellis, as we head back to the Range Rover.

What a fucking rush...

See, can't beat a good old fashioned ruck, better than any drug you'll ever take. Like everyone else, I'm walking on air as I'm buzzing so much...

As we head back to 'our' side of the river, the calls start coming in…

The bragging begins…

I hear, who's knocked the shit out of who, who 'met Stanley', that's as in the well known workman's trusty tool of a retracting knife which has its very own rep. I even hear about a few meat cleavers and machetes being used… *No, I am not shitting you… I told you, this firm of mine are fucking nutters.* I'm just glad there were no shooters. It was a good old fashioned hooligan fight, with a few blades and bottles, which is standard for something like this.

By the time I'm back at the club, I know, who's in hospital having treatment. It varies from concussions and stab wounds, to an endless array of fractures and stitches.

It's as we are having a few celebratory lines, Paulie Parker starts asking if we saw the geezer with the sword?

"What fucking sword," I laugh as pinch my nose. "You're still buzzing mate, a fucking sword?" I wink.

"Nah man, you should have seen it, *cunt* pulled it out of its sheath," we look at him. "I seen one, on TV, innit… At me Nan's… On the history channel or whatever?" He looks to us.

"What? She likes all that kind of shit, innit... Reminds her of the olden days." he looks around the room as we pull the piss out of him. "Looked proper and all.... I'm not fucking with ya."

"*Proper* and all, even with a sheath Paulie?" I look at him mockingly, eyebrows raised in surprise. He gets all excited.

"Yeah Gov, shiny an all it was, I saw him swinging it around his head, like he was in Zulu or something," with that, we all fall about laughing.

All in all, today has been fucking magic, couldn't have planned it any better... I am well chuffed with the outcome of today's events and we won at the game too... Smashed on and off the field... Take that you muppets...

The festivities of the evening, are that of the champions we are. We head downstairs to the club and the girls. We take one of the private backrooms and have an array of girls sent in.

It's as one tasty tart is grinding into my lap I spy Tommy at the threshold of the door.

Poor, Tommy, him, being the pal he is, he's obviously worried for me since hearing about this hit business. After the tart has finished I go over to talk to him.

"Tommy," I nudge him jovially. "Cheer up geezer, we are officially the '*Top Firm*' in London... Fuck, the *UK*... As if **I** didn't know that already."

I smile proudly at the boys, raising my bottle of lager to them as a salute.

But he don't have to say anything, I know that look. It is one I am *very* familiar with, I've caused it enough times... *FEAR*!!

"Tommy, you worry too much," I throw my arm around him. "Don't be a worry wart... I swear *your* Mrs. must have your cock in her bedside drawer or something," I laugh, as I admire the dancers still gyrating on the lads laps. "Can you even for one night, just chill the fuck out?" I motion with my head in the direction of the fun and games. "Why don't you go and sit down and have some pussy rubbed on ya cock, get yourself all charged up so you can go home and bang the Mrs.?"

He looks at me, I just give him one of my reassuring smiles and walk him over to the booth and pop him down.

Immediately he has a beautiful brunette rubbing herself on him. She grabs his hands and places them on her tits as she does her thing.

Remember, this is my club, normal rules don't apply to my boys.

The banter in the room is unbelievable, the coke and pills are as plentiful, as is the pussy...

It's like paradise in here, well it is for the lads, but not for me...

Yeah, you guessed it, I'm thinking of '*Her*'. I know, *what the fuck right?*... Here I am, top of my game, beautiful women shaking their tits and pussies at me... And I'm still thinking of '*Her*', enough to make me check my phone.

I see she has responded to my message. An image of '*Her*' face flashes into my head. All I can do is think of her. I think back to all those stolen looks we had over the years. *I know, I got it bad...*

Enough that I slip upstairs to the privacy of my office under the watchful eye of Big Dave, who promptly stands guard outside my door. I shake my head laughing at him in bewilderment, as I start to dial '*Her*' number. As if anyone is going to kick off with me tonight... *Tonight I am invincible!!*

Before I hit call, I make my way to my desk and prepare a couple of lines... I am still charged, the adrenaline is coursing through me from the ruck today. It's just as I finish the second line that she answers.

"Do you know what bloody time it is?" I hear her bark down the phone.

"Well... Hello to you too," I chuckle. "And *no*, what time *is* it there?" I smugly say as I swing my feet up onto my desk and relax.

"Well, we are 8 hours ahead of the UK..."

See, see that? Never a straight answer, always something to get you thinking, although this time she *is*, actually trying to get me to think.

"Okay," I chuckle. "Whatever... So what ya wearing?" *'She's'* right, I'm incorrigible.

"A business suit, like every day *I work*" she laughs. "You'd like it... It's perfectly tailored... Anyway, what's up? You're lucky you caught me, as I'm just finishing off my coffee before I head out the door to a meeting."

"You still working with them American's? Any of them try it on with you yet?" I hear her laugh, well, it's more a scoff.

"Not everyone is a raving whore like you, *you know*... Of course *not*, these gentlemen are professional... Not like *some people* I know."

"Do I hear a little hint of sarcasm in your tone?" I ask, trying to be serious, even though I'm containing the laughter.

"No... *LOTS* actually." She laughs before she then starts to tut. "*Hardman*, you know I never '**do** *anything* little'," she purrs, teasing the fuck out of me.

"I *swear*," I laugh. "You wait until I see you,"

"*Ooh*, now I'm intrigued as to what you'll do to me," she purrs, with just enough seductiveness, that I feel my cock go instantly hard.

"Let's just say," I look to the tent pitching in my trousers, shaking my head. "I am really looking forward to seeing you," I chuckle.

"How much?" She coos.

"About nine and a half inches much," I laugh, rubbing the tip of my crown with my thumb over the cloth. *Yeah*, I'm imagining it's her tongue, teasing my helmet.

"*Mmmmm*, shame I have to go to work, why don't you ring me later?"

"But it's a Sunday there innit?! I ask surprised. "Surely you're not on the clock... Don't you get a day off? Fucking slave drivers or what?" I hear her laugh at the other end.

"I'm a translator, it's why I am here... They have functions to go to and I have to do my job... Girls got to earn a buck you know," she purrs. "Anyway, I really have to go, the car is waiting for me downstairs and I can't keep these chaps waiting."

"You've kept me waiting long enough," I chuckle.

"As much as I would love to talk filth to you, I really have to go..." 'Her' tone is softer. "Call me later yeah?"

"Only if you say it?" I tease.

"It," she coos, then laughs.

"Say it, say you're mine," I growl as though I was growling it in her ear. I hear her giggle again.

"I have to go," she laughs.

"Say it and I'll let you go," I tease.

"It," she sniggers. She can hear me scoff. "Okay, okay, you're not going to let me go unless I do, are you?"

"Nope," *see* how I'm not budging.

"Okay, I'm yours," she mocks, sounding monotone. "Is that okay?" She teases again. *Me*? I am actually chuckling at this. "Okay, well call me later yes?"

"Yeah?" I try to sound pissed off.

"Oh and Hardman?"

"Yeah," I answer.

"I'm yours..." And she hangs up...

I sit there, big, cheesy grin on my boat, I'm like the cat that got the cream. What a perfect end to a perfect day...

That is, until I hear raised voices coming from the other side of my door...

"What the fuck is going on out here, I can't hear myself think?" I stare at Kelly. "What you doing here?" I look at her blankly. "I thought you was with Daisy now?"

Now, in hindsight, the smirk was probably a bit too far, to a woman scorned.

"I only wanted to come in and see you, that's all," she tries to flutter her fake eyelashes at me.

"As I said," I look at her coldly. "I thought we were done," and I purse my lips together.

"Why... Who are you fucking now?" She starts screeching like an alley cat.

"You what?" I look to Big Dave shaking my head, as he shrugs his shoulders. "What the fuck are you banging on about you dozy mare?"

"You got someone in your office?" She tries in vain to look over my shoulders. "Who, who is it? Who's in there?"

"What the fuck are you on about, you bint?" I look to Big Dave, who shrugs his shoulders again. "Do me a favour?" Kelly looks at me. "And *fuck off* will ya."

Defo the wrong thing to say as she punches me hard in the face.

Immediately I grab her jaw and throw her against the wall. My fingers clench on her skin.

"I'm going to let you have that one," I lick my lips as I snarl. "I probably deserve it in your eyes," I squeeze her face tighter as she winces. "But if you come at me again like that... I'm gonna put you down like a geezer... You got that?" She nods her frightened head. "You want to give it the big-un and throw punches like a man, I'm gonna treat you like one... Got it?"

I let go of her and she scarpers away like a little mouse. I look to Big Dave.

"What the *fuck* mate?" He gives me one of his dumbass looks. "You can't even handle a bird," I chuckle shaking my head as I walk back into my office.

I pick up the phone and dial down to the bar and call Tommy up.

Minutes later I hear Tommy's knock and in he walks. I motion for him to take a seat and pull out two glasses and the bottle of scotch from my drawer.

"No, you're alright Gov," he waves his hand. "Don't like the stuff," he pulls a soppy face. "Don't agree with me, gives me heartburn," and he rubs his chest in a circular motion. I take no notice of him and pour him one anyway.

"You're getting old Tommy," I smile as I raise my glass to him. "And so am I..." I place the glass back onto my desk and look at him. "It's time for me to walk," his face says it all. "Yeah, I bet you thought you would never hear them words coming from my mouth," he nods his head, his mouth still aghast with shock. "But yeah... Done it all now, 'My Firm' are **the** '*top dogs*'... I'll be going on a good note."

"A legend, among legends," he reaches for the glass I poured for him and raises it in the air to me. "To your good health," he smiles proudly at me.

"Yeah... It's *time*, I suppose" I recline back in my chair. "Here, listen to this for a laugh... I just had that 'Kelly with-the-tits' up here,"

Tommy looks at me clueless.

"Took a swing at me," I scoff, before shaking my head at her nerve. "Nice choice by the way, just my type," he smiles smugly at me. I however, change my tone.

"... But you knew that, didn't you Tommy, knowing me as long as you do.... And... There's the icing on the cake....What with finding out... That fucker Freddie... Was with *'Mad Dog's' sister*?" I look at him, I want answers. "*Tommy*," I stare at him calmly. "You're normally on the ball... I was looking at keeping this place open," I sip from my drink again, my eyes never leaving his. "*Naturally*, it was a no brainer... **You** were going to run the club... That was, if you were up for it?" I still maintain eye contact. "Now... What I want to know is... *How did*, something like *that*, get past *you* Tommy?" I still eyeball him and place my glass down. "You have your ear to the ground... Nothing *ever* gets past *you*." poor Tommy's eyes nearly fall out of his head

I see Tommy shifting very uneasily in his chair.

Now, what Tommy don't know is, that when I was reaching into the drawer to get the drinks, I also got my gun...

And... It's pointed at *him* under the desk...

"So, explain it to me Tommy boy?" I keep my focus and call out to Big Dave, who immediately comes into my office. "Why Tommy?" I shake my head woefully. "I've never seen you wrong... I always looked after you. Never saw you short... *Ever*!" I look at him. "I thought you were the loyalist fucker there was," I breath hard. "*Why*?"

He goes to say something, but nothing is coming out of his mouth. What can he say?
But it don't matter. I can't sit here and listen to him trying to talk his way out of it... He knew the score when he started doing what he did. My 'personal business' was with my accountant.

He was the one that noticed something was wrong, had his eye on it for a few months. That's how we caught Freddie...

But, to say I'm shocked that it was Tommy behind this *all*, is just sickening for me. I never saw it coming. I feel rightly double crossed.

"D, do me a favour, call Leroy and Ellis up sharpish will ya on your mobile?"

He nods his head, unaware of the conversation me and Tommy just had and pulls out his phone and calls them. In no time at all the two are in my office.

Meanwhile, Tommy is still sitting in the chair, sweating bullets, no doubt shitting himself.

"What's up Gov?" Leroy nods as they come into my office, both of them stand behind Tommy, arms folded.

"It appears we have a problem," I then look back to Tommy, as I raise the gun up from its concealed position.

They say nothing as they step forward and reach swiftly, each grabbing Tommy under the arms lifting him clean out of the chair, dragging him backwards out the door as Tommy tries to reason with them. *Silly Tommy*, **he** of all people should know better than that.

He is taken out of the club by the back stairs, bundled into the back of a car and they are gone.

Everybody is totally unaware of the situation and that's how it will stay.

I toss the gun back into my drawer and slam it shut. I sit there numb, unable to move.

My stomach is in my mouth... *Not Tommy?*

Out of everyone, it had to be *him*?

I had my suspicions it was someone close, but finding out it was Tommy, is an absolute kick in the nuts...

I'm gutted...

I down the rest of my glass, pour another and neck that. Before I realise, I am grabbing for my bin and I puke into it. I drop the bin to the floor sitting back wiping my mouth. I quickly pour another drink, knocking it back...

It's not everyday you send one of your oldest friends to their demise...

15

WALK

I sit there for a good few hours, I don't even notice when it starts getting darker. I look at my phone and message her, telling her to 'contact me urgently' and wait...

It takes her an hour, I know it is, as I checked the time I sent it, when she messages me back. Telling me *'She'* was sorry, she was held up in a meeting and to give her fifteen minutes.

So I wait...

I dial her number and let it ring.

"It was Tommy," I feel like the wind has been taken out of my sails.

"Oh *God*... No... *Ohh Hardman*," her voice is soft, full of concern. "*I'm so sorry*."

"I'm gutted," I feel my head shaking, with anguish.

"Of course you are," she sighs, empathising with me. She knows how long me and Tommy go back. "Do you know why?"

"Because he's a greedy back stabbing cunt," I spit. "That's why," I am full of anger, sorrow and remorse intertwined in one.

"I don't know what to say?" She feels my pain.

She's heard enough stories about my antics with Tommy over the years. He was such a huge part of my life... And I can say 'was', because Leroy and Ellis have just parked up their car. I hear the engine turn off, confirming it.

.

I don't know what to say, I feel utterly lost. I really didn't think it would be him. I thought it could have been one of the 'On duty Bar Managers' and was watching the shifts... But Tommy?

I don't know what to say, but with her, I don't have to say anything, just being able to do this is doing the job.

"*God*, I wish you were here," I exhale heavily.

"If it helps, so do I," she breaths

"I hate your job," I grumble.

"I hate *yours*," she tries to laugh. "More than you hate mine, *believe me*."

"*Yeah*, have to agree with you there," I'm lost for words again. "Still, I *do* wish you were here."

"Well, not long to go now, you only have to wait until Tuesday... That's if you don't melt again," she giggles mischievously.

"Don't start that Harlow," I chuckle, I can feel the smile form reluctantly on my face. *See*, see what '*She*' does to me?

"Just saying," she teases me again.

"Yeah, yeah," I go silent again.

I can't get the image of Tommy's face realising that I was on to him. I've seen the face of a condemned man many times... But *his* is one I will *never* forget...

It will forever haunt me, that is why the time is right. I've had enough, Tommy's deceit was the straw that broke the camel's back for me.

"So, have you any idea of where we can meet up on Tuesday?" Her voice breaks me out of my deep thoughts.

"Yeah, I have a few places in mind... And we talk first yes?" I laugh, I know exactly what's coming next, and being honest, I need her doing this right now.

"*Oh*," She sounds disappointed. "Shame, I was just thinking we may talk after... I mean, what if you're really shit in bed?"

"What?" I splutter.

"I mean, what if you're just all mouth and really not that much action... Would you buy a car without test driving it first?"

I can't answer, as I am laughing so much.

"I'm not committing to anything until I've had a test drive... What if you turn out to be one of them lemons?"

"A lemon?" I'm still chuckling.

"Yes... And not the bitter yellow one either," she has a tiny chuckle, before she continues with her charade. "You know, that would be just my luck... You are getting old now you know, there may not be many more miles left on the clock if you get my drift," *see*, even using my phrases to really stick it to me. "Anyway, I think once you and I are left to our own devices... Do you really think we will talk?"

"You have a point there," I agree. "So, what are you going to do to me?"

"I'm going to devour you *Charlie Hardman...*"

"*Mmmmm*, sounds good... Tell me you're mine," I demand.

"Hardman... Don't start," she giggles.

"Say it... Tell me you're mine."

"You're incorrigible," she laughs.

"Never been in dispute... Say it."

"It," she curtly replies.

"You wait," I tease.

"Gonna have to wait until Tuesday I'm afraid. I have to go... Another meeting, but I'll text you when I'm out, should be for only a couple of hours. I hate going, but I have too."

I know normally we wouldn't be speaking while she is on the clock. But she knew I needed her and she came through.

"Yeah, I'll catch up with you later. Message me when it's cool."

"Will do, speak to you later, sorry I have to go, but if it helps... Tuesday."

And she's gone, leaving me in my dimly lit office. I look at my watch, it's the early hours of Sunday morning, still dark outside.

It's time I went home to Connor and Rita, I have to sort out that first, before I can do anything else now.

As I walk out of the office, I see Big Dave sitting on a chair. I forgot he was still outside.

"Sorry D," I look at him, shaking my head remorsefully at him. "I completely," He interrupts me.

"Not a problem Gov," he looks at me.

He knows the score, he knows what happened with Tommy. Like me, he's shocked, but he's been around long enough to know that you live by the sword, you die by the sword. The look on his face says it all. He knows how hard that decision was and how necessary it was. We have rules and Tommy was trusted, he got greedy and his respect is no more.

I don't know what to say. As you know, I don't have clean hands... There is a bar tab in hell with my name on it. But being honest, I'm lost for words.

"I'm heading home," I stuff my hands in my pockets and start to make my way down the stairs to the club.

It's too soon for me to use the back stairs.

I hear Big Dave following me, it's only when we get to the bottom that I turn to him.

"D, go home," I place my hand on his shoulder. "It's been a long day," I purse my lips in thought. I know I look mardy, but under current circumstances, allowed.

"Nah Gov," he looks at me solidly. "Nah, ain't going anywhere, without you," and he looks me deadpan in the eye.

"Yeah alright," I toss him the keys, I'm in no mood to drive either.

We walk out the back to the Range Rover, get in and make our way back to my place. We say nothing on the drive to the house, we don't even have the radio on. Actually, we look like the solemn chaps we are. Big Dave pulls up into my drive and parks the car. I turn to him before getting out.

"Why don't you come in D," and I motion with my head. "Better than being out here all night," I shrug.

He accepts, nodding the once and out we get.

He knows my gaff well, been around here quite a lot, to the point I was thinking of charging him rent. So I know he's sound being here. He knows where he sleeps, so all is kosher.

I walk up the stairs straight into Connor's room. He's fast asleep, I kiss him goodnight and make my way to the master suite. I see Rita is out for the count on a concoction of sleeping tablets and gin. I laugh to myself, she is such a cliché for a gangsters moll.

Don't get me wrong, she is a lovely girl. But she's in love with this lifestyle... The money, the drugs, the clothes, the cars and the status of being in the position she's in. I tried ending it with her a few times, however, she's a fucking nightmare, and believe me, that coming from my mouth is serious.

But she is Connor's mum, even if she is a shit one. That is why I come home, to make sure my boy is okay. old nanny type live-in housekeeper. She has her own granny-flat and can keep an eye on Connor when I'm not there.

So now you know the score with my Mrs. who's not even my Mrs. by marriage.

I head into my walk-in closet, undress and make my way to the steam room.

There I can think about how I'm going to broach talking to her about ending us. I spend half an hour in there and then hit the shower. I dry off and head into bed with the comatosed Rita. If we had an earthquake, she'd sleep through it, knowing how she doses herself up.

I lay there thinking how happy I am to be walking away from all this, the big swanky house, the constant nagging of Rita, work.

I close my eyes, but all I can see is Tommy's face. I toss and turn, before deciding to get up and go to my home gym. My mind is racing ten to the dozen. I'm asking myself why Tommy got greedy, I always looked after him. He even had a house up the road from me and believe me when I tell you, I live in a nice part of London on a private road with security.

I walk into the gym when my phone rings, I look at it to see it's Tommy's Mrs. 'Maureen'. I am not looking forward to this. I turn on the gym music system and answer. I stand under one of the integrated ceiling speakers so she thinks I'm still at the club. I tell her Tommy left the club hours ago, *see*, no lie there and also that I haven't spoken to him since he left.

She knows the score and doesn't push me any further, but that is a loose end that will need tying up.

I know her and the kids will have to be looked after and *we will*. It's not her fault Tommy fucked up and I am godfather to their eldest and youngest, so it's my duty.

I'm in the middle of warming up when my message tone goes off. This means '*She*' is free to speak and me being me, I'm gonna ring her.

"Oi, oi," I hear as she answers. "You okay?"

"Yeah, I'm at home."

"Ohh, I'll, erm," she stammers, '*She*' don't like this situation, I can tell.

"No, it's cool, fast asleep, if I shook her, she'd rattle, she's taken so many pills," I force a laugh.

"*Still*," I hear the hesitancy of her. "Not right is it... I'm the one who looks bad here, even though you're a raving whore."

"How do you make that out then?" I lean against the wall shaking my head at her old fashioned ways.

"Well, officially, you're with Rita?"

"It will be sorted in the morning," I answer.

"Wow, that soon?" I hear she is shocked.

"Yeah, I've wasted enough time and this home situation isn't good for Connor."

"*But*?" She tries to defend.

"Nah, kid has seen too much, she's not exactly mother of the year."

She knows I've tried and she understands what I mean. We both have abandonment issues, I've stayed here this long because I didn't want history repeating itself, with a parent walking out because they couldn't take it anymore. It's why we go above and beyond for our kids, give them what we never had. But I don't want *this* for my son, I want him growing up in a good positive relationship and dare I say a loving one, which should be the case.

"*But still*," I can imagine her shaking her head at all of this, it's not sitting right with her.

"Don't worry about all of that, that's my shit," I scoff. "It will be sorted because I wanna be with you innit?" I try to lighten the mood. "Look don't worry. I'll call you in the morning, it will be night no doubt for you."

"Yes, okay then," she sighs.

"Trust me... I'll sort this, you and me will be having a different conversation tomorrow, trust me yeah?" She knows I mean business. "Message me before you go to bed yeah?"

"Okay, okay, I'll speak to you, *your* morning then."

"Don't worry... Night," I'm being positive. "Call ya tomorrow."

"Night then," and she is gone.

I don't feel much like lifting weights now, as I feel the tiredness start kicking in. I let it win as I walk back to the master suite, get into bed and close my eyes thinking of what I'm going to say to Rita...

The morning comes too soon. I have tossed and turned for most of the night, so I haven't had much sleep. I get up and shower, after that, I pack two bags, one for me and one for Connor. I'm not leaving him here, a moment longer.

I head into Connor's room and wake him up for breakfast. I know Mrs. Beven won't show her face until 9am, it is Sunday after all. Big Dave, will also get up after that and he'll potter around as normal, seeing he feels at home here.

I make a point of us eating at the breakfast table, it's our ritual. I make him a good ole mans breakfast, a full English with all the trimmings.

I look at him, like I do every morning and wonder how lucky I am to have him and for us to have the relationship we do. And I work at it, spending quality time with him.

Connor will never have a taste of the life I lead. I've never even smacked him, never needed too, he's a great kid. Never gives me a moment of trouble, does really well at school and everything.

To say I am proud of him is an understatement.

After our food, we spend some time on one of his computer games, which he annihilates me at and not because I let him either. Before long Mrs. Beven comes in and starts pottering around.

I ask her to take Connor out, so me and Rita can talk. She's more than aware of Rita and the situation we are in, it's the reason she's here after all.

So we arrange for her to take Connor out after 12pm, seeing as Queen Bee, won't be up until after 1pm, regardless of what day of the week it is. Gives me an hour to talk to 'Her' before I speak to Rita.

We have a good talk, well, more me telling 'Her' hopefully, what the future will entail. I am feeling good about the talk, that I'm gonna be having with Rita.

The others in the Harem, they'll get calls. As far as I am concerned, after today, I'm not going through any more woman drama after speaking to Rita.

... And that's gonna happen now, seeing I can hear her moving about...

16

FEELING A MOMENT

Rita eventually makes her way downstairs. She's still dressed in her silk pyjamas and matching kimono, which as per usual, is not tied up, as the sash of the belt hangs limply in its hoops.

Her hair is probably as near perfect as when she went to bed, judging by the shares she must have in a 'hairspray company' with her usage.

She says nothing as she passes me and heads into the designer kitchen.

I hear her moving around, no point in going in after her, as she'll be back in after she has poured herself a Sunday morning breakfast glass of proscecco.

And sure enough, in she comes flouncing in and slumps down in one of the designer Italian armchairs and starts to sip from her glass.

Big Dave is in the Den, watching some block buster movie on the home cinema, so I know we won't be interrupted.

I let her have at least half the glass before I start to talk. No point otherwise, she wouldn't be with it. It's like coffee for her.

"We need to talk," I look at her.

"About what?" She motions with the glass at me.

"I'm leaving… And, I'm taking Connor," she goes to talk, but I carry on, ignoring her. "You can have the house, it's all yours and the car. I'll give you an allowance," I see her eyes widen.

"How much?" I know she's surprised.

But it's hard to tell with the amount of Botox she's had in her, to know facially that she is.

"Enough, that you won't even know we're gone," I watch her as she casually sips without a care in the world.

"I thought we were going to wait until Connor was older?"

"Rita, we can't do this," and I motion with my hands. "No more… It's toxic," I shake my head. "It's not a good environment for him," I shake my head with disgust. "I have all the paperwork ready, so if you sign this, you are sorted."

I reach into my breast pocket, taking out the envelope containing the papers I need her to sign. She don't batter an eyelid, signs them like she had won the lottery, and was collecting her cheque.

"So when are you going?" She hands me back my pen. "Oh, that's a point," she looks around, still drinking her proscecco. "Where's Connor?"

"Out with Mrs. Beven," I get up and walk towards the stairs. "We're gonna go when they come back," I lean my hand on the banister.

See, that's her level of parenting, and she thinks she is brilliant.

I head up and grab the bags and bring them downstairs, leaving them at the foot of the staircase. I don't see the point in staying a moment longer. Connor and me can stay in a hotel until we leave. I have him enrolled in one of the English schools aboard, private of course.

I head into Big Dave and tell him my plans about leaving the country. I tell him, he always has a place with me, if he wants to come.

Big Dave is single and his only ties are me. He is more than happy with my offer, so I am a happy bunny. I message Mrs Beven and tell her the coast is clear and to bring the lad home. All I have to do now is wait for Connor to come home and we are gone.

15 minutes later they arrive home, and without a second look back, we go.

I check us into a hotel, not too far from the club. Unfortunately, Mrs Beven can't travel over with us, but will stay until the end of the week, when we leave. Shame, as Connor really likes her, but she has family here, it's understandable. I'm just grateful, she'll be with us until then, means I can tie up all the loose ends that need doing.

Big Dave and me, head back to the club. Connor is happy, the suite has a huge TV and a gaming system, so he's content being there.

Big Dave parks the Range Rover up and we get out. I stand there and look at my club. It has good memories… And bad.

No, I am not thinking about Tommy. He got what he deserved, like all them scum bags.

We head into the club to be met by Leroy and Ellis. They both have a look on their faces, I know they want to speak to me. But it's Leroy, who does the talking for them.

"Gov," they look between themselves then back to me. "We need to talk," I look at them and nod.

They follow us up to my office and close the door behind them as I sit behind my desk, while Big Dave waits outside the door.

"Gov," they exchange looks again. I sit there patiently. "He said something before," and they look uncomfortably between themselves again.

By the looks they have on their boats, it ain't good.

I have a knot in my stomach knowing I am gonna be hearing Tommy's last words.

"Before," and his eyes widen. "You know," and his eyes widen again, like he don't want to say the words; '*We killed him*'. "*Well*, he tried to plead, saying give him time," I roll my eyes. "Well, he said," and they look between themselves again. I brace myself for it, but they stare between themselves, beckoning each other to say it with their eye and head movements they are doing.

"Will one of you fucking say, what you have to say?" I look sternly at them both.

"He wanted to buy time by making a call," I look at them and shake my head, exhaling loudly. They know they are pissing me off 'big time'. "To the Hitman *he* hired."

"Okay," I look at them. "*And*?"

"Well, of course we didn't," Leroy shrugs his shoulders. "We thought, buying time," and he looks to Ellis, who's nodding, agreeing with him. "It's just, me and Ellis are thinking, **should,** we have let *him*?"

"Nope," I shake my head. "*No* boys, you did the right thing. You know a man will say anything to buy himself some more time. If I was in the same boat… I would have done exactly the same," and I motion with my hand. "No mercy."

They look relieved, in fact very relieved as they breathe easier. I am impressed with their loyalty, although, thinking about *this 'after the event'*, isn't exactly very helpful to me right now.

I thank the lads and they go, leaving me to my thoughts.

At least I know now, who put the hit out on me and Tommy knows all my contacts for a job like that. All I have to do, is to find out *who* has taken the contract and make them an offer they can't refuse.

I make a few calls and leave the ball rolling for information, it shouldn't be too long, before I have a name I can work with…

I go about my business and Sunday flies by. I avoid all the calls from Tommy's Mrs. Maureen. This isn't a biggie, I do it quite often, as did Tommy, especially when he occasionally went on the missing list on a bender with a bint he liked. So all is normal.

I try and make contact with '*Her*', leaving her a message. And as normal, I play the waiting game with her to get back to me.

The evening rolls on, I get a message back saying '*She's*' in a meeting, but will message me when she is free. So all good.

By late evening 'She' messages me and I call her.

"Oi, oi," I smile, proudly, knowing I have news for her.

"Hello," I can hear her smiling as she says it. "How are you?"

"I'm good… Very good in fact... We left the house today."

"*Wow*, shit," she is speechless.

"She signed the paperwork like I knew she would," I can hear her take a breath, ready to say her piece. "Before you say anything, I told her, that the house and car were hers and she has an allowance… She wouldn't even notice we are gone."

"How did she take that?" I know '*She* is shocked.

"Nearly bit my hand off to sign the papers," I sigh, This is the point when I think of how *easily she gave up Connor for the money.*

"He can never, ever know she did that Hardman, that would damage him, forever... *We* know what's it's like to be rejected... But when it's your *own* mother?" She sighs heavily. "Poor Connor, how is he?"

"He's as happy as Larry, hasn't a clue what she's done and *he never will.* He's back at the hotel with the nanny," I like the fact, even though she hasn't met him, she still shows more concern for him than his own mother does. Over the years she has seen his pictures, so it's not like she don't know what he looks like. And she's heard enough about him over the years, seeing I do like to brag about my boy. "So, all I need now is for you to get your arse over from China, to me," I purr.

"Wow, I'm still shocked you've done all this," *I bet she is,* I'm thinking.

"Told you... I want you, I've waited long enough… All my ducks are in a row and all I need is *you* here, at *my side*."

"You have it all worked out then?" She laughs.

"Yep, final piece of the jigsaw is you… So, roll on Tuesday," I smile to myself, knowing, I've just got Monday to go until she is here…

We talk for about an hour, then as usual, she has to go.

But it's all good. I've only one more day to go, then, she is *mine...*

I walk out my office to see Big Dave, he follows me down to the club. It's late, but the place is packed as usual. I start to make my way out to the back and a minor altercation occurs between a waitress and an over friendly punter , just as we pass.
I take no notice, continuing on my way as the waitress pushes the twat, he stumbles into Big Dave and starts giving all the large-un.

It's as I hear the door close behind me I hear it...

"Well, well, the 'main man' himself," I hear a gruff voice behind me.

I wait until I reach the bottom step to turn around. The way I see it, I wouldn't have heard or known a thing if he didn't want me to see him so he can gloat.

"Terry Butler," I look at him. "So I take it *you're* the guy then?"

Terry has rep for being a complete nutter, it's one of the reasons the army kicked him out, dishonourably I'll add. That was after three tours of duty. He's a crack shot, and is one of four people you would call to do a job like this. Guy has no soul, taking a human life to him, is like killing an ant. Oh, and yes, naturally my sources called, but the thing is, me and Terry don't see eye to eye on a number of things...

"*I am*," he smiles smugly. "Gave them a discount, when I heard *your name*," and I see the diamond he has in his front tooth twinkle from the light above the backdoor.

Fucking typical, getting taken out by a classless fucker, who has a diamond set in one of his front teeth... I mean, who does that now?

"Okay," I say nonchalantly. "It is, what it is," I tilt my head as I shrug. "So, you gonna do it here?"

I watch him slowly walk down the three steps to join me. He was standing behind the door, waiting for me. His handgun is steady in his hand as he joins me. I'm watching his eyes...

Everything is in the eyes... You look closely and you can see everything, like when they are going to make a move, and that is what I am watching for...

Now, I need to point out... *Yes*, it's a bad thing that Terry is in front of me, pointing a gun in my face... *However*, what I find worse is the fact this cunt feels he is compelled to give you a fucking ritualistic lecture, on why he is here. And so he starts...

"Charlie... Hardman... *Nothing* gives me, the greatest of pleasures, than to be standing here, in front of you tonight," he grins at me.

He is such a *sanctimonious cunt*, it's not funny. And due to the gun aimed at me... I have to fucking listen to it *too*... I'd rather have the bullet at this rate.

"You know," he laughs mocking me. "I really didn't think I would enjoy this as much as I am... and I *really* am Hardman," he flashes his diamond tooth like the twat he is. "In fact, I'm delighting in this moment altogether."

"Oh for fuck sake," I look at him. "Just pull the fucking trigger and get on with it will ya... It's bad enough having your name attached to me, never mind having to listen to you prattle on like a fucking bitch on her period," and I look at him blankly.

"*Okay*," he smiles as he raises the gun from my chest to my head. "Have it your way..."

CRACK!!

I watch, as Big Dave comes down the stairs, in complete silence with a pick-axe handle clenched in his huge hands, while Terry waffles on like that geezer in 'Pulp Fiction'. He raises the wood ready to strike...

... And he does. *HARD* on the back of his nut and knocks the fucker clean out, sparko.

Terry hits the deck and the gun goes flying, skidding across the floor...

Big Dave stands there, wide eyed, the pick-axe handle , still posed ready for another swing if necessary.

"Gov," he shakes his head. "*Fuck*, I'm sorry. I don't know how the fuck I got caught up with that?"

"Big Dave," I smile at him. "Never have I been so delighted to see you mate... You were here when it mattered," I purse my lips together, nodding his chivalry. "Perfect timing if you ask me."

"What do you want doing with him?" He slings Terry over his shoulder, just as Leroy and Ellis come bounding out the door and towards us.

"Get rid," I look to them as they all nod.

Leroy and Ellis walk with Big Dave to their car and Terry is thrown into the boot. Leroy and Ellis, gag and tie the fucker up with cable ties, while Big Dave makes his way back to me.

I look around and I see Kelly, standing near the dumpsters having a sneaky fag. She walks towards me, however, I ignore her and meet Big Dave. I really can't be dealing with her shit right now.

Being honest, my heart is still pounding in my chest and I want to get back to Connor. I know Kelly is calling after me, talking, but me and D get in the Range Rover and drive off, leaving her standing there...

"What a fucking night?" I look at Big Dave, thankful that he came when he did.

I'm shocked. For a big mother fucker, he was incredibly light on his toes.

We get back to the hotel and Connor is asleep in his room . Mrs. Beven , Big Dave and I all have our own ensuite rooms. We say goodnight. Big Dave heads into his and I into mine.

Before I shower, I receive a call from Leroy and Ellis. The Terry 'predicament' has been resolved and is no longer an issue. *So, all good there.*

Before I settle in for the night I text her seeing if she is around. To my surprise, she is and I call her.

"Oi, oi," I smile hearing '*Her*' voice, it's good to hear her, after what's just happened.

"Hello, how are you, how has the rest of your day been?" I can hear the concern in '*Her*' tone.

Now here is where I chose, *not* to tell her what happened tonight… *Especially* as it will freak her the fuck out. Plus… Situation, isn't an issue anymore, so, it will keep.

I listen to her talk, and then hear something recognizable.

"Is that an *announcement?*" I hear a Chinese bird speaking over a tannoy system.

"Yes, I'm *err*… I'm flying back from one province to another," she says hurriedly.

"*Nice*... Another step closer to being here then, yeah?" I laugh.

"Yes, it is," she coos. "Look I have to go, they *really are* calling my flight."

"Well, happy flying," I tease.

"Yeah right, you're funny, very funny," she mocks still laughing. "Well, have to go, it's the last call, I'll see you soon. Take care."

And she is gone...

I close my eyes, believe it or not I'm happy.

Me and the boy have left Rita, the Queen Bee... I've avoided certain death, standing face to face with Terry Butler. But thankfully, due to the ever faithful, Big Dave, I am still here... Plus, '*She*' will be here on Tuesday... Roll on Monday.

Monday morning arrives. I order breakfast for us all to be sent to the suite. I'm nagging at Connor to hurry up. It's good I suppose, as it gives him some form of routine.
I'm not in too much of a rush, what with being closer to his school and all.

So we leave nice and relaxed. I'm feeling pretty positive about life or rather the thoughts of our new one. I drop Connor off at school and head off doing my normal Monday thing. It's funny as I go from business to business, knowing it will be my last time doing all this. After all that, it's early afternoon when I head back to the club.

It only opened an hour ago, and there are still, the hangers on from the lunch time trade. I make my way across the club to the stairs that lead up to my office. That's when I hear a very familiar voice behind me.

"Oi, oi," I turn and see '*Her*' sitting at a booth. She stands up smiling as she walks towards me.

"What the?" I stand there, glued to the spot. I shake my head in disbelief, as I start to walk towards her. "*Jacquie Harlow…* What the fuck are you doing here?" I can't believe my eyes.

"*Nice*," she scoffs shaking her head sarcastically. "I jump on a plane, a day early... *And* this is the greeting I get?" She shakes her head again regretfully. "*Yeah*, that wasn't how I saw *this* going down," she still shakes her head still, faining a wounded look.

"Then how's about this one then?" And I place my hands gently either side of her face and pull her to me and kiss her like I've never kissed anyone before.

It's a long and sensual never ending one, and *yes*, my cock is raging hard because of it. From the moment my lips touched hers I knew everything would be perfect.

I pull her closer to me, adoring her lips, devouring her with kisses until we both remember where we are. We pull away like two teens caught by the parents.

"Hmmmmm," she pulls a perplexed face. "Actually... I've **had** better," she smirks up at me like the cheeky minx she is.

"Have you *now*?" I look at her, watching the devilment of flames burn wild in her eyes.

"I have," she looks at me indignantly.

With that, I pull her to me again, as we devour each other once more. Personally, I've never been so delighted to see *'Her'. Fucking bonus or what?*

We're still in the throes of a passionate embrace, when I hear someone clearing their throat.

I spin around, whoever it is, is gonna get their head fucking ripped off.

I will tell you now, I never saw this coming...

"Who the fuck is she?" A demented Kelly motions with her head.

"Seriously?" I look at her, bewildered. "What the *fuck* are *you* doing *here*?"

"I said... Who the fuck is *she*?" Kelly's voice gets louder, more demanding. "Tell me?" Now, she's gone into shriek mode. "Is this *who you* chucked me for? *For her?*" She looks over at '*Her*'. "How old is *she* anyway?"

"I beg your pardon?" I hear '*Her*', pipe up.

"You heard Grandma," she scoffs, giving her dagger eyes.

I hear Jacquie, say 'charming' as she laughs under her breath looking Kelly up and down.

"Kelly," I shake my head at her, this situation is *fucking nuts*... "*Look*, you need to calm yourself down love," I'm trying to be reasonable here, plus, remember, *always on my best behaviour for her*, it's what she deserves.

"You fucking her too?" She is losing it a bit here now. "Were you fucking us both at the same time?" Kelly rants.

Yep, she is really losing the plot now.

"Look Kelly, you're a lovely girl, a smashing girl... But we're over love... It was fun... Hey, it was good fun, yeah?" I try to reason with her.

Nope, I really didn't see this coming at all. Mind, you, I do have Tommy's words of women trouble in the club, echoing in my ears.

"You kissed her?" She looks me in the eye, her eyes are black with rage. And she repeats it again. "You wouldn't kiss me... *No*... I'm only good enough to shove your cock into my mouth, down my throat, up my cunt, ain't I?"

I sigh heavily, I really don't have time for this... And I don't really need Jacquie hearing all about this again.

"Do you love her?" She looks at me and screams it again. "*Do you LOVE her?* **You** had your eyes shut!"

With that, she pulls out a gun. I look at it, as she raises it up and points it at Jacquie.

It's Terry's gun!!

Of course it is... How could **we** *have missed it?*

Then I remember this dozy mare having a sneaky fag by the dumpsters, where the gun slid when Terry dropped it.

You can imagine, I'm having a bit of an epiphany here, remembering how the Terry event unfolded...

And now, this stupid bitch has a gun aimed at *us*...

"Put it down Kelly... Before someone gets hurt," I slowly move towards her, my hands in a peaceful stance. "You don't want to hurt anyone, do you?" She's waving the gun between Jacquie and me

"Answer me?" She demands, now the gun is aimed firmly at Jacquie. "Do... You... **Love her**?"

"*Yes*," I look back at Jacquie. "*Yeah*... I do..." I smile at '*Her*' before turning back, to face this nutty tart. "But Kelly?" I inch closer. "She's the innocent one here," I move nearer. "*Kelly*," my voice is calm. "She hasn't a clue what is going on," I watch her eyes as they dart between me and Jacquie. I need her to see sense.

"It's *me* you want to hurt," I tap my chest, she looks at me. "*Yeah...* **Me**... *Not her... It's me you want,*" I carry on tapping my chest, keeping her focus on me.

I watch her slowly nod with recognition, agreeing with me.

"So put the gun on me... *Yeah*?" I inch closer and closer as she darts the gun between me and Jacquie again, her eyes are wild with fear.

As I negotiate, I spy out of the corner of my eye, Big Dave sneaking out from the staircase doorway.
In his hands, *you've guessed it*... The pick-axe handle and he is closing in behind her.

It seems, Kelly is watching my eyes too and she senses something is wrong. It's either those famous women senses... Or, it could just simply be, Big Dave's shadow moving towards us. I suppose it's hard not to see, seeing he's a monster.

The gun moves between me and Jacquie the closer I get. But I want her focus to stay on me. I can see Kelly's hand is shaking.

Samantha Fontien

She knows she got to be quick and she will have to do something, because she was already warned...

So she knows what is coming... And it will be HARD.

"That's it... Me, *me...*"I slap my chest, keeping her attention. "The *cunt* who *fucked* you over my desk, *yeah?*" I nod, trying to goad her.... "Shoot me and you'd better be quick," I see she is getting jittery, accidents happen in times like this. I have to keep her focal point on me. "But I will tell you this *you dozy tart*... Do it quick... *Coz I'm gonna make* retribution **hard** for you... I promise you that" I look at her, my face snarling with anger.

Her hand is shaking like a leaf, her bottle is going, but that gun is still moving between the two of us, she is a wild card.

"Yeah, **me**..." I slap my chest again, egging her on. "Shoot me... *Go on... Shoot me....*"

"Okay then," Kelly looks blankly at me as she calmly shrugs...

It's funny how life is...

My life right now is moving in slow motion. I see the gun being fired and I hear a sickening thud and cries of *'NOooooo'*...

I stand there, as I watch Big Dave and Leroy make for Kelly, tackling her to the floor, in slow motion.

Once again, the gun goes sliding across the floor. My hearing has suddenly intensified, I hear everything like echoes. I turn and look at Jacquie, who has tears in her eyes, crying out *'NOooooo' as* she runs to me...

Then, things move slower. I stand for a moment, before falling to my knees. I've taken my hand away from my stomach and I'm looking at it.

Its caked in blood... I look down at my white shirt and it is turning redder by the second...

Spreading fast...

I fall forward just as Jacquie gets to me and falls to her knees as she cradles me. I can taste blood in my mouth.

This can't be happening?

I look up and I can see *'She'* is frantically calling for help.

But I can hear nothing now and I'm getting weaker by the second as the life drains out of me.

I feel '*Her*' touch my face, begging me to hold on, well that's what I think she is saying. I know I have people around me, but all I want to see is '*Her*'.

"Connor," I mumble.

I see Jacquie shaking her head, full of worry, her face is streaked with tears as she calls for help...

But the black is coming...

Suddenly I am feeling afraid... I try and hold on to her, but I have no strength in me, the darkness is coming for me...

I can see her lips moving...

She is telling me 'she loves me', over and over again. To hold on...

I don't know if she can hear me, but I am telling her 'I love her... It's always been her'...

And everything goes black as I fall into darkness...

I feel nothing!!

I can't see, but I can hear...

I hear beeping noises...

Slowly, I open my eyes, to find Jacquie asleep in the chair next to my bed. I look over at her and being honest... It's the loveliest vision to see when you wake up in a state like this. I hurt all over.

She senses I'm awake and jumps up, happy to see my eyes finally open, judging by the amount of kisses she is planting on me.

Apparently, I've spent four days in the ICU. I should have one more day in here, and if all goes well, I will be moved to a regular private room.

Waking up and seeing her there is magical, really is. I even get a hard-on, *so*, thankfully, that all seems to be working okay.

After the Doctors and nurses leave, having checked me out. '*She*' explains to me what happened after I was shot.

Kelly was held by Leroy, seeing that Big Dave wanted to tear her apart with his bare hands. She screamed like the loony she is, even when the old Bill turned up.

They came and arrested Kelly. She is currently undergoing some desperately needed psychiatric evaluation.

Jacobs, of course, was first on the scene. I'd say he will be well fucked off to hear I made it.

... I don't give a fuck about him though... He can '*Do one.*'

Big Dave is standing outside the door. I watch as Jacquie tells him to come in. The smile on his boat says he is very happy to see me.

We have a little private chat and he highly approves of Jacquie, telling me she virtually hasn't left my side. That sort of makes me feel great being honest with you. I knew she loved me all along.

As for me?

I'm apparently going to make a full recovery. I should be out of here by the end of the week if all goes well.

Then, Jacquie, Connor, Big Dave and myself, will be gone, sunning ourselves at my spacious villa.

So, life is good and that's what I'm planning to be...

Good that is... They deserve it, *fuck*, I owe it to myself and them. I have everything to live for...

'If you live by the sword, you die by the sword'...

So... I'm hanging *mine* up.... **Permanently,** with Jacquie... I am no longer *'Active'*.

I've been lucky in lots of things... *However*, I've been given a second chance... Not only in love... But, also life... And I plan on doing both to the full, with my family...

I'm going proper legit, in *everything*. Gonna ask Jacquie to make an honest man out of me...

And...

... I'm gonna love it...

The End... *or is it?*

Note from Jacquie…

I know you must think I'm mad?

Maybe I am?

But it's always been '*Him*'. I've never been able to get him out of my head, hence why we spoke so much.

Even when I went out with him for that drink, so many years ago, I knew '*He*' was the one. He made my heart bang in my chest like a drum, along with my panties too, like no one else ever has.

.   I knew it also the day I married my ex-husband, who I would class as the perfect man template...

But he wasn't '*Him*'...

...'*Charlie Hardman*', the boy who teased me and made me cry. He was a horrible bastard at school and I tried to have as little to do with him as possible. However, I always caught him looking at me, but he was so angry all the time, well that's how I saw it. Plus he started to have a reputation for being a naughty boy. I know some girls like all of that, but not me.

Nope, I've had enough crap in my life, never mind bringing it full force, like only the likes of '*Charlie*' could.

God knows I've tried to keep away, the same as '*Him*'. It's like we're drawn together like magnets.

They say fate is a funny thing and it really is.

Throughout our lives, we have crossed each other's paths. I have been in some of his circles, hence me, not wanting anything to do with it.

With everything I have been through, I need stability in my life. *And Charlie was too wild...*

Don't get me wrong, I love Hardman's wild side, it's one of the reasons '***we***' get on so well. '*He*' knows how to make me tick in all the right ways, he's a pure animal and we tend to be a bit to primal when conversing. He's right, we do 'sense our own'.

You're probably thinking I am all prim and proper... *I am*. I've worked bloody hard to pull myself up, to achieve the lifestyle I have.

But what you don't know about me, is I am naughtier then Hardman. My sexual tastes are more...

Let's just say, I've experienced things that Hardman has only dreamed of doing. I know this is also huge turn on for him as well.

You see, I don't want to tame Hardman, I want him like the wild animal he is… I just don't want his 'gangster lifestyle'.

'*He*' is a clever chap, always was, I just wonder what the right education and environment would have done for him if he had, had the right start in life.

I really only knew Hardman like I do now, when we started talking a few years ago and he started opening up to me. It blew me away, I gained a new found respect for him. I saw him in a completely new light.

To me, Hardman was always the template of 'What I didn't want' **or** 'look for' in a man. We have always been friends and could always talk about anything and often did. But that night, when we properly started to share 'our secrets', the spark ignited and never went out.. I know I get the best of him, I see him like no other, bar Connor of course. Believe me when I tell you he really is a man of honour and very deep, like an ocean. He intrigues me greatly and he behaves himself too. Believe it or not, he is always a gentleman around me.

The way I see it, Hardman's right, it's a gamble. I can walk away at anytime. Well, that is what I am telling myself. I still haven't met a woman who can resist his charms.

So, I'm taking a chance on Hardman, finally...

Either way, I have to get him out of my system... One thing I do know, how much I regretted not kissing him, but I couldn't then.

I had been with my ex for years at that time and it just seemed a bit uncouth being honest... Plus, I didn't want to be a notch on Hardman's bedpost. He had a terrible reputation for it.

But when he talks about Connor, I see another side to him. Connor's such a lovely boy and my heart goes out to him. The poor lad was a pawn as far as Rita was concerned. I've never met her and I wouldn't want to. Having a child is a gift, not a bargaining chip and I've lived that life, so I know how that feels.

I myself can't have children, it's one of the reasons bar Hardman, why my marriage failed. After a few rounds of IVF treatment, we soon realised we weren't right for each other.

I knew when Hardman called me about Tommy, I needed to be there for him. I knew how much it ripped him apart. He is as proud as I am. Tommy and he, were old secondary school friends, they came up through the lines together, shared everything.

This is another reason why I don't want any part of that life.

I hope Hardman can stay free from it, if not, he knows I will walk, whether I want to or not. I won't live that kind of life.

I know how he's achieved his money, there is nothing I can do about it. It is what it is. As long as that is the end of that, we'll be alright.

I also knew Kelly would be a problem. I told Hardman this when he first mentioned her. She had 'Class A bunny boiler' written all over, from the word go.

However, I do feel sorry for her, Hardman gets under your skin very easily. He has a way of connecting with you, always has. He was always a right proper chancer and also very, very charming indeed…

'A right proper Charlie.'

He's been very aptly named.

I knew how I felt about '*Him*', when I got on the plane to come back. But seeing Kelly pointing the gun at us, just helped to affirm how we felt.

Funny, it took a gun and this life of his, for us to say how we really felt about each other and after so long playing games.

Well... Now, I can actually say; '*He*' took a bullet for '*me*', he '*loves me*' that much...'

How many women do you know, that can say that?

The End...

COMING SOON
KRISSY V

THE SWEET GIRLS OF
WHISKEY SOUR

*Where The Girls Are Sweet, But Their
Dancing Is Not!*

Whiskey Sour is an unusual place for such a
diverse group of women to meet. It's a very classy
burlesque club in London's Soho! You'll find the
most amazing women whose dancing is sensual,
sexual and beautiful. Each of them have their own
style and their own story to tell. You are invited to
come along and meet each of the 'Sweet Girls of
Whiskey Sour' and find out the journeys they have
been on to become the women they are now.

Whiskey

Comes from the school of hard knocks. She is a
sassy, headstrong woman, who becomes a mentor
and confidante to her burlesque dancing protégés...
However, she battles with her own secrets, which
she has buried forever. Fed up of running away
from everything, she decides to stand up and be
counted. Her philosophy is "What doesn't kill you
makes you stronger!"

Whiskey Sour is her salvation and it soon becomes a refuge for women who need rescuing from one nightmare or another.

Zephyr

An 'A' student who moves to London to study as a lawyer. She has to work to pay for her studies and after several jobs Whiskey approaches her in a club after seeing her captivating dancing. She offers Zephyr an opportunity which changes her life ... in more ways than one...

Snow

Is an elegant, classically trained, ballet dancer who has the potential to become a 'Prima Ballerina'. After coming home from a world tour to find that she has been betrayed by the one person she loved the most, she has to start her life all over again... After a chance meeting with Whiskey, she soon becomes 'Whiskey Sour's' favourite girl.

Betsey

Betsey's convinced she was born in the wrong decade. She spent her young life watching wartime movies, wanting to be like all the 'beautifully chic' leading ladies... So now she is.! .. She's the 1950's all day ... every day. It's her life! 'Whiskey Sour' is her home, where she can finally be accepted for her quirkiness.

Blue

Streetwise Blue is a hip hop dancer who has come from dancing on the streets to sleazy clubs... Now, she works in the safe surroundings of Whiskey Sour. She helps Zephyr to integrate into the Whiskey Sour family and they soon become best friends.

Pinkie

Pinkie is a self-confessed 'Posh bit of totty'. She has her own style of dance, dress and attitude. She comes across as a bitch, but underneath all of that front is a very insecure woman who just wants to be accepted into this amazing world she finds herself in.

Raven

She is the newest member of the Whiskey Sour troop. She was always a dreamer and at sixteen she ran away from home to join the circus. With them she lived and breathed performing, travelling the world until tragedy strikes in more ways than one causing her life to change. When she is introduced to Betsey, her life starts to swing in the right direction.

OTHER BOOKS BY SAMANTHA FONTIEN...

HOW TO CATCH BUTTERFLIES
BOOKS 1 & 2.

THE DRAGONFLIES TRILOGY

THE DUNCAN PETERS FILES. #1
THE RIZZO PROTOCOL. #2
COUSINS – THE NEXT GENERATION. #3

WEE BOOKIE OF NOOKIE
(NOVELLA SERIES)

A DIP IN THE FONTIEN.
FROM A TO B.
A TASTE OF TURKISH DELIGHT.
BACK IN BLACKWALL
(COMING 2016)

ALL AVAILABLE ON EBOOK AND PAPERBACK

~ALL PLAYLISTS AVAILABLE ON SPOTIFY~

* THESE BOOKS CONTAIN DRAMA, HEARTACHE AND MATURE
CONTENT, INTENDED FOR READERS 18+ *